Surviving the City

Tasha Spillett

Natasha Donovan

HIGHWATER
PRESS

Canada Council   Conseil des Arts
for the Arts   du Canada

We acknowledge the support of the Canada Council for the Arts.
Nous remercions le Conseil des arts du Canada de son soutien.

HighWater Press gratefully acknowledges the financial support of the Province of Manitoba through the Department of Sport, Culture and Heritage and the Manitoba Book Publishing Tax Credit, and the Government of Canada through the Canada Book Fund (CBF), for our publishing activities.

HighWater Press is an imprint of Portage & Main Press.
Printed and bound in Canada by Friesens
Design by Relish New Brand Experience
Cover art by Natasha Donovan
Lettering by Donovan Yaciuk
Anishinaabemowin (Saulteaux) translation: Jerry Sumner

Library and Archives Canada Cataloguing in Publication

Spillett, Tasha, 1988-, author
        Surviving the city / Tasha Spillett ; Natasha Donovan.

Issued in print and electronic formats.
ISBN 978-1-55379-756-2 (softcover).--ISBN 978-1-55379-784-5 (ebook).--
ISBN 978-1-55379-785-2 (PDF)

        1. Graphic novels. I. Donovan, Natasha, illustrator II. Title.

PN6733.S65S87 2018   j741.5'971   C2018-904204-4
                                                    C2018-904205-2

22 21 20 19   2 3 4 5 6

HIGHWATER
PRESS

THE DEBWE SERIES

www.highwaterpress.com
Winnipeg, Manitoba
Treaty 1 Territory and homeland of the Métis Nation

For our girls,
and the land living beneath the concrete
that remembers they are sacred.

And for the women,
seen and unseen,
who hold up the sky.
—T.S.

For my best friend, Sky – thank you for your love.
—N.D.

Little Sister

Little sister
I see you even if you have yet to see yourself
Even if you mask yourself in fragments of untruths of you
Even when you cloak yourself
because somewhere, sometime, someone has made you feel that to hide
is safer than to shine as you were meant to

Little sister
I wish to speak into your mind sacred words of you so loudly that they
are like the Thunderbirds when they come to visit
and wash everything away
I wish to make you a crown of sage to show to all that rest their eyes on you
that you are made of medicine and of royalty

Little sister
I will sing songs to you until your voice remembers that it was meant to dance
I will pray into being all that is needed to remind you
that you are where beauty and strength come together to embrace
I will dance medicine into the path that we walk on so that is again safe
for you

Little sister
I see you

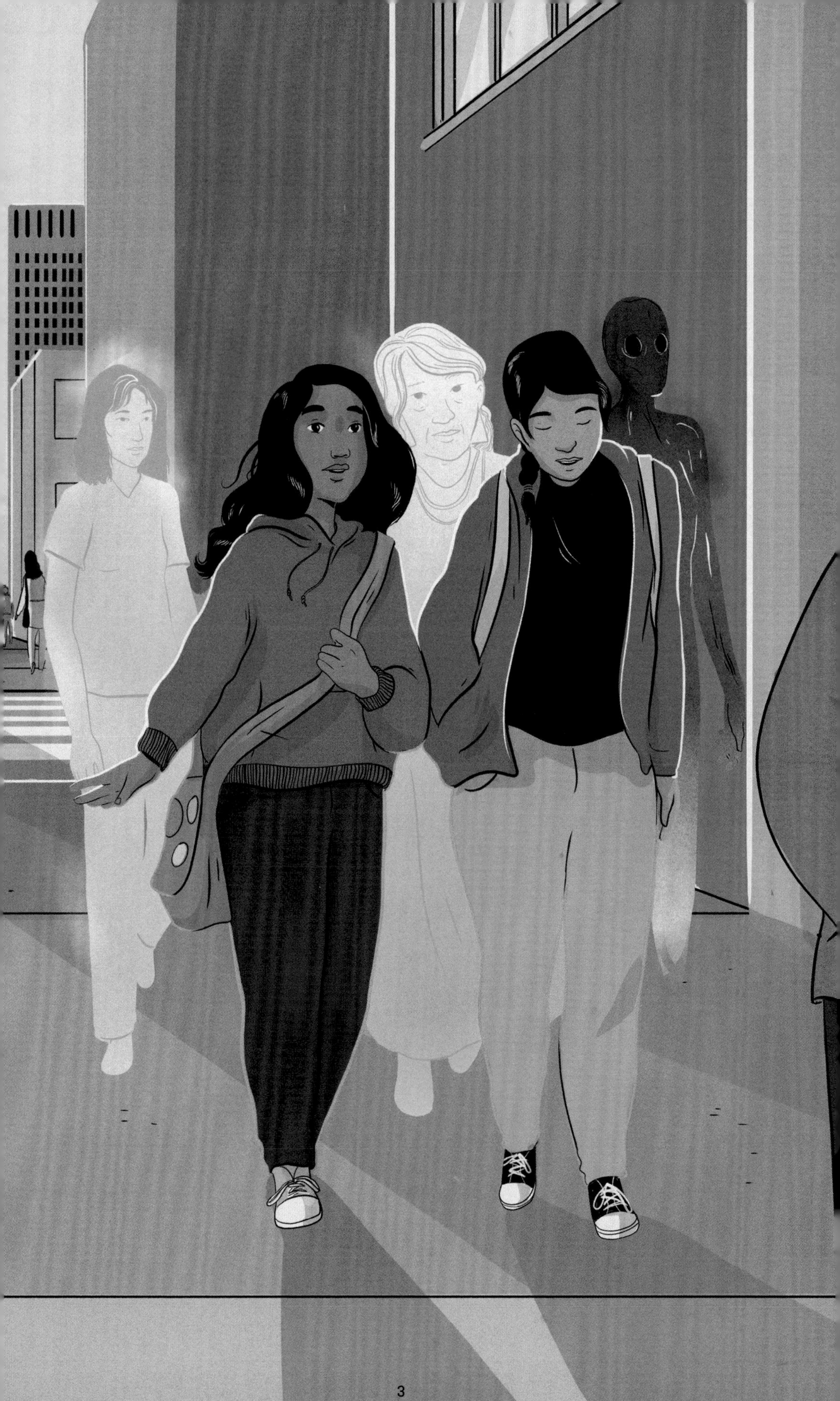

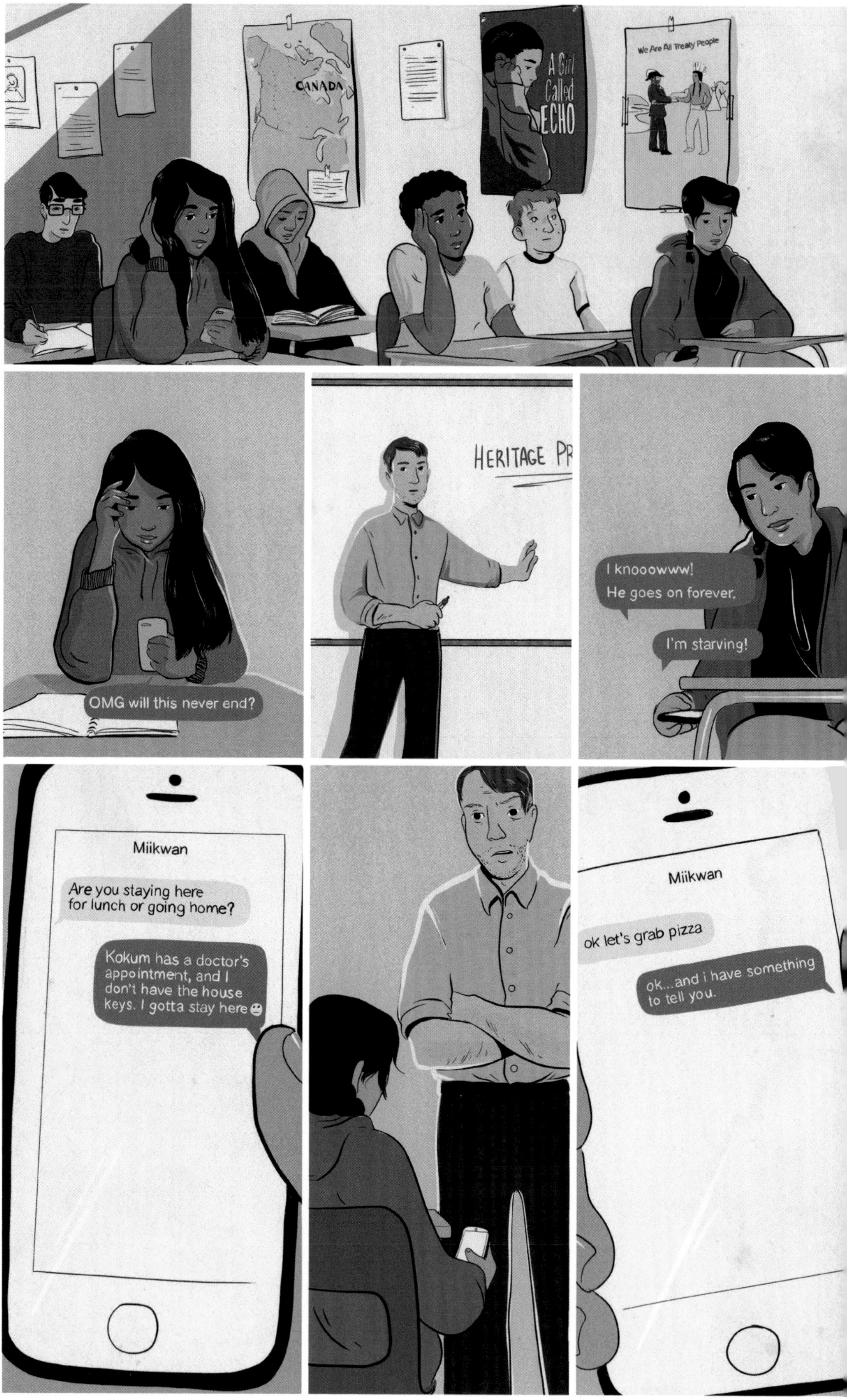
CANADA
A Girl Called ECHO
We Are All Treaty People
OMG will this never end?
HERITAGE PR
I knooowww!
He goes on forever.
I'm starving!
Miikwan
Are you staying here for lunch or going home?
Kokum has a doctor's appointment, and I don't have the house keys. I gotta stay here
Miikwan
ok let's grab pizza
ok...and i have something to tell you.

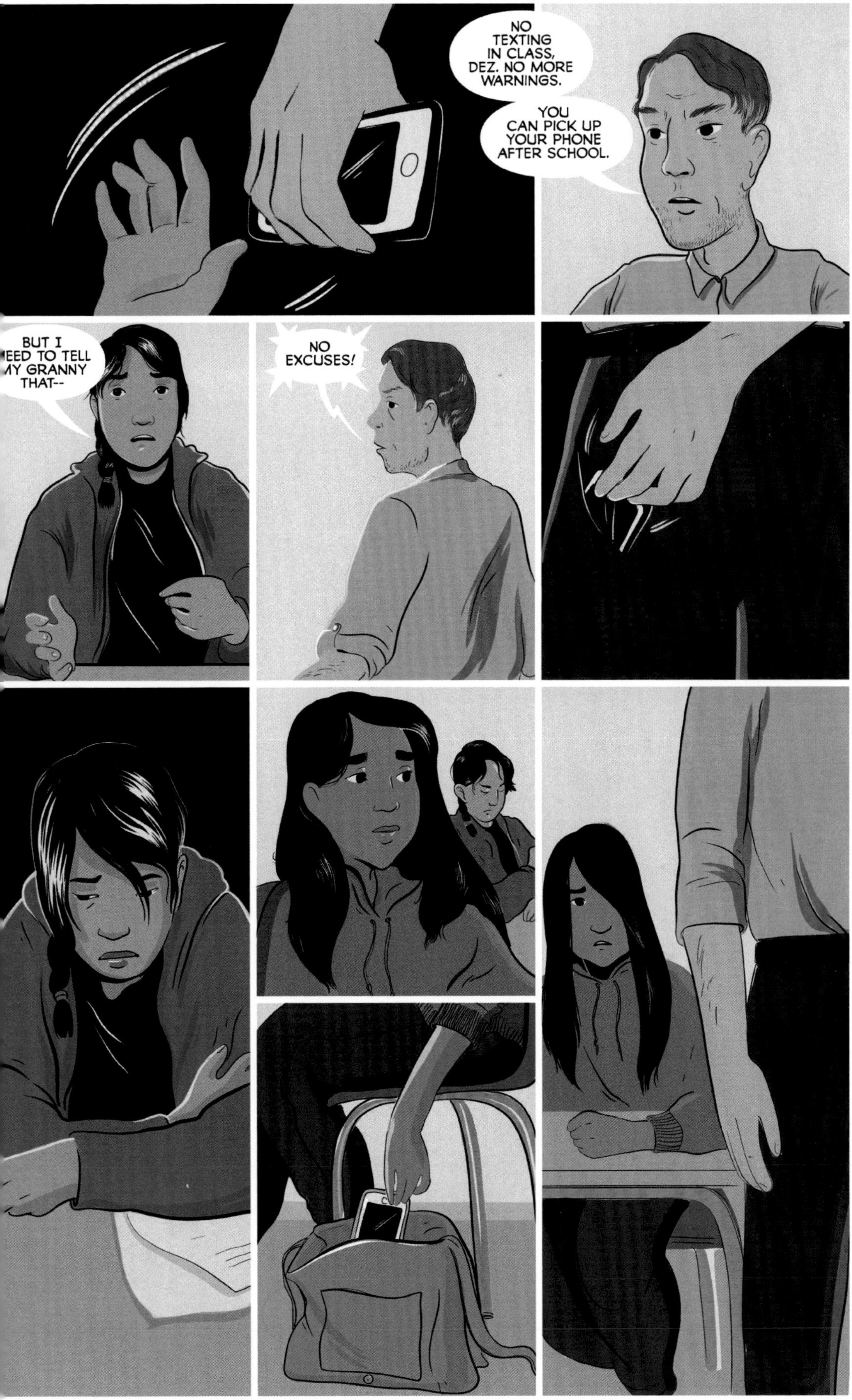
NO TEXTING IN CLASS, DEZ. NO MORE WARNINGS.
YOU CAN PICK UP YOUR PHONE AFTER SCHOOL.
BUT I EED TO TELL Y GRANNY THAT--
NO EXCUSES!

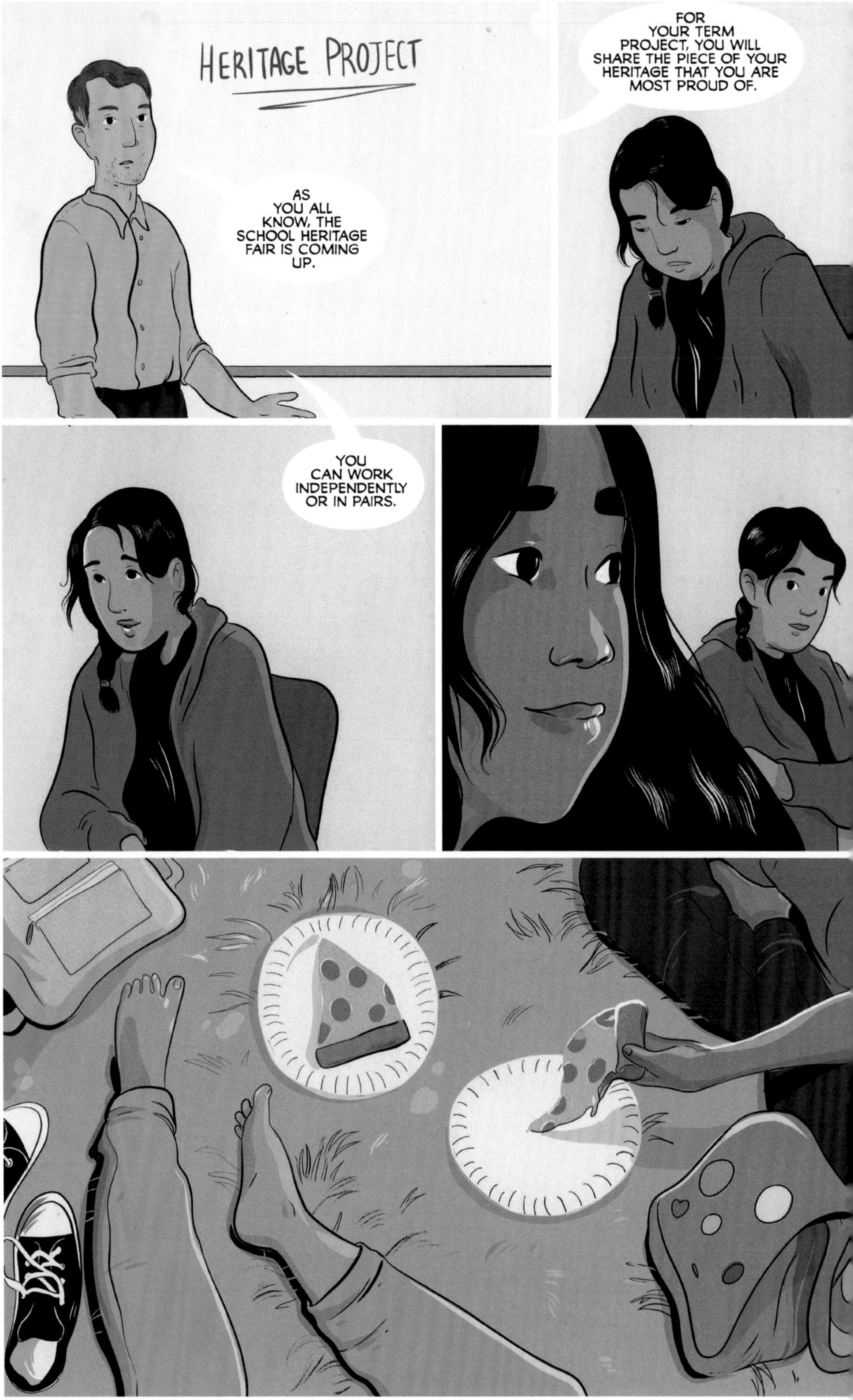
HERITAGE PROJECT
AS YOU ALL KNOW, THE SCHOOL HERITAGE FAIR IS COMING UP.
FOR YOUR TERM PROJECT, YOU WILL SHARE THE PIECE OF YOUR HERITAGE THAT YOU ARE MOST PROUD OF.
YOU CAN WORK INDEPENDENTLY OR IN PAIRS.

#FreeDezsPhone

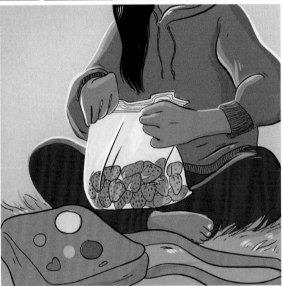

OOOOO BERRIES!! AREN'T YOU SO HAPPY WE CAN EAT THEM NOW?

REMEMBER HOW HARD IT WAS TO STAY AWAY FROM STRAWBERRY SHAKES AND HAVE PB AND J WITH NO J, FOR A WHOLE YEAR!

OUR *BERRY FAST!* THAT'S WHAT WE SHOULD DO FOR OUR HERITAGE PROJECT.

THAT'S PERFECT! WE CAN TAKE ALL THE PICTURES FROM OUR CELEBRATION FEAST OFF FACEBOOK.

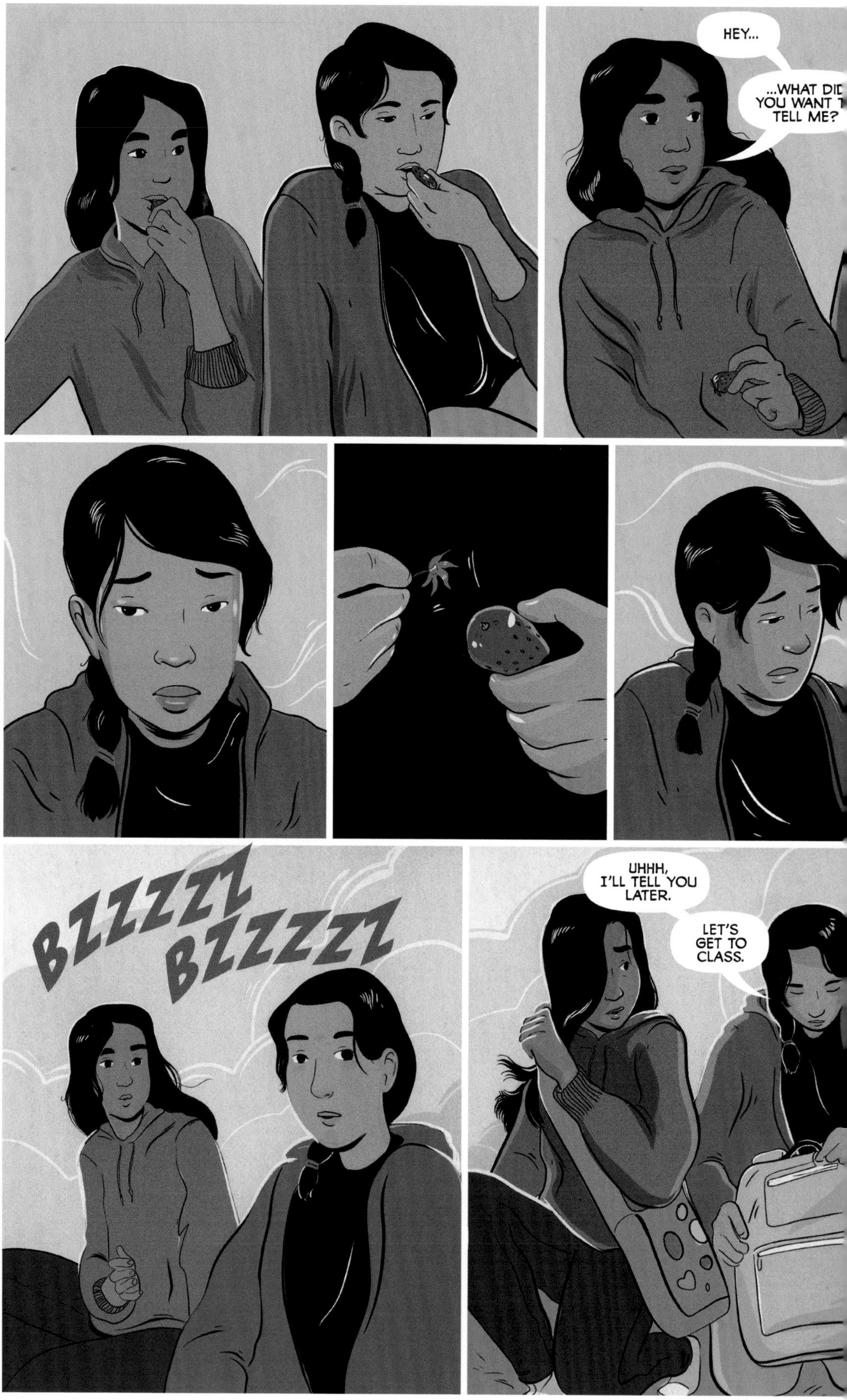
HEY...
...WHAT DID YOU WANT T TELL ME?
BZZZZZ BZZZZZ
UHHH, I'LL TELL YOU LATER.
LET'S GET TO CLASS.

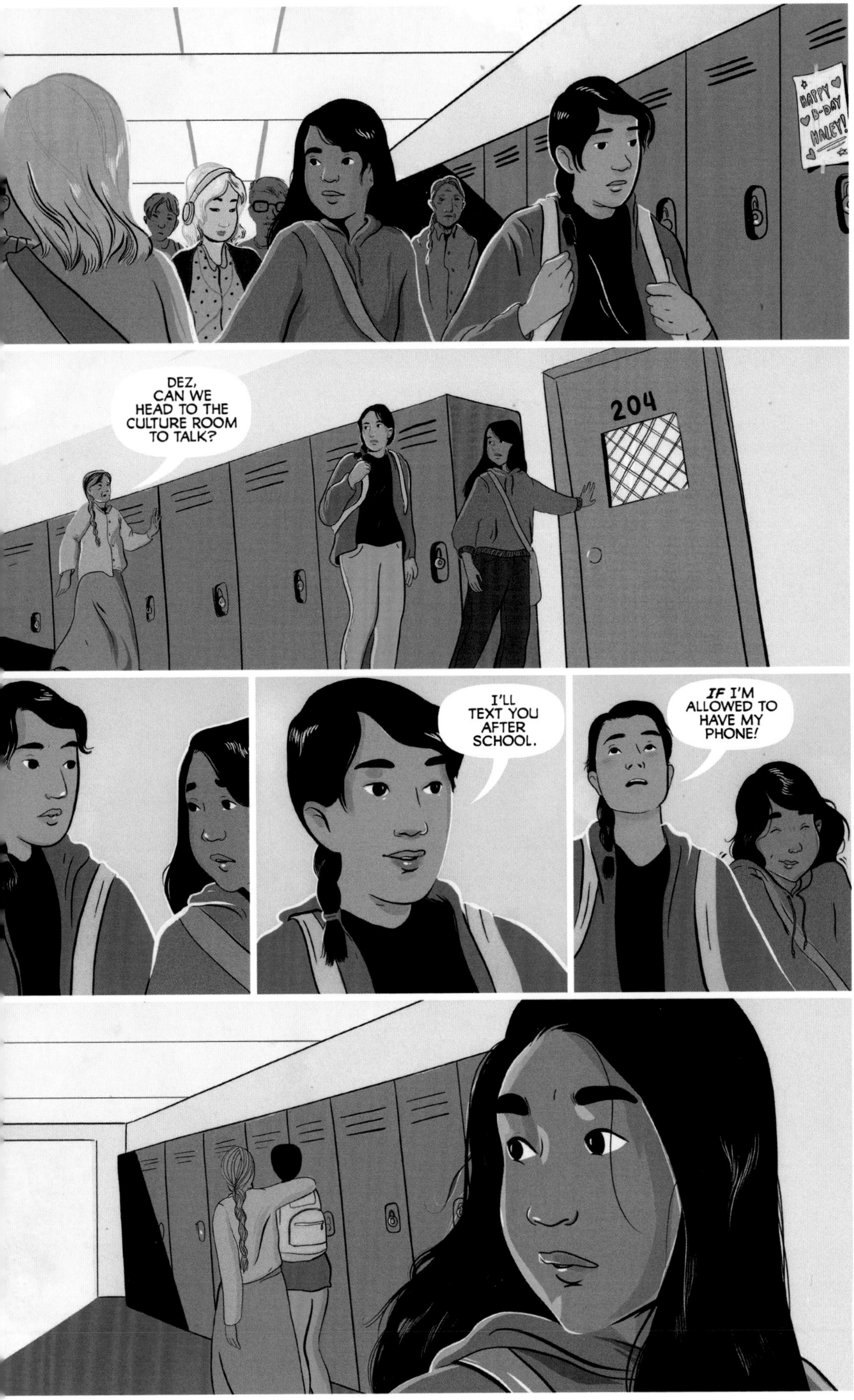
HAPPY B-DAY HALEY!
204
DEZ, CAN WE HEAD TO THE CULTURE ROOM TO TALK?
I'LL TEXT YOU AFTER SCHOOL.
IF I'M ALLOWED TO HAVE MY PHONE!

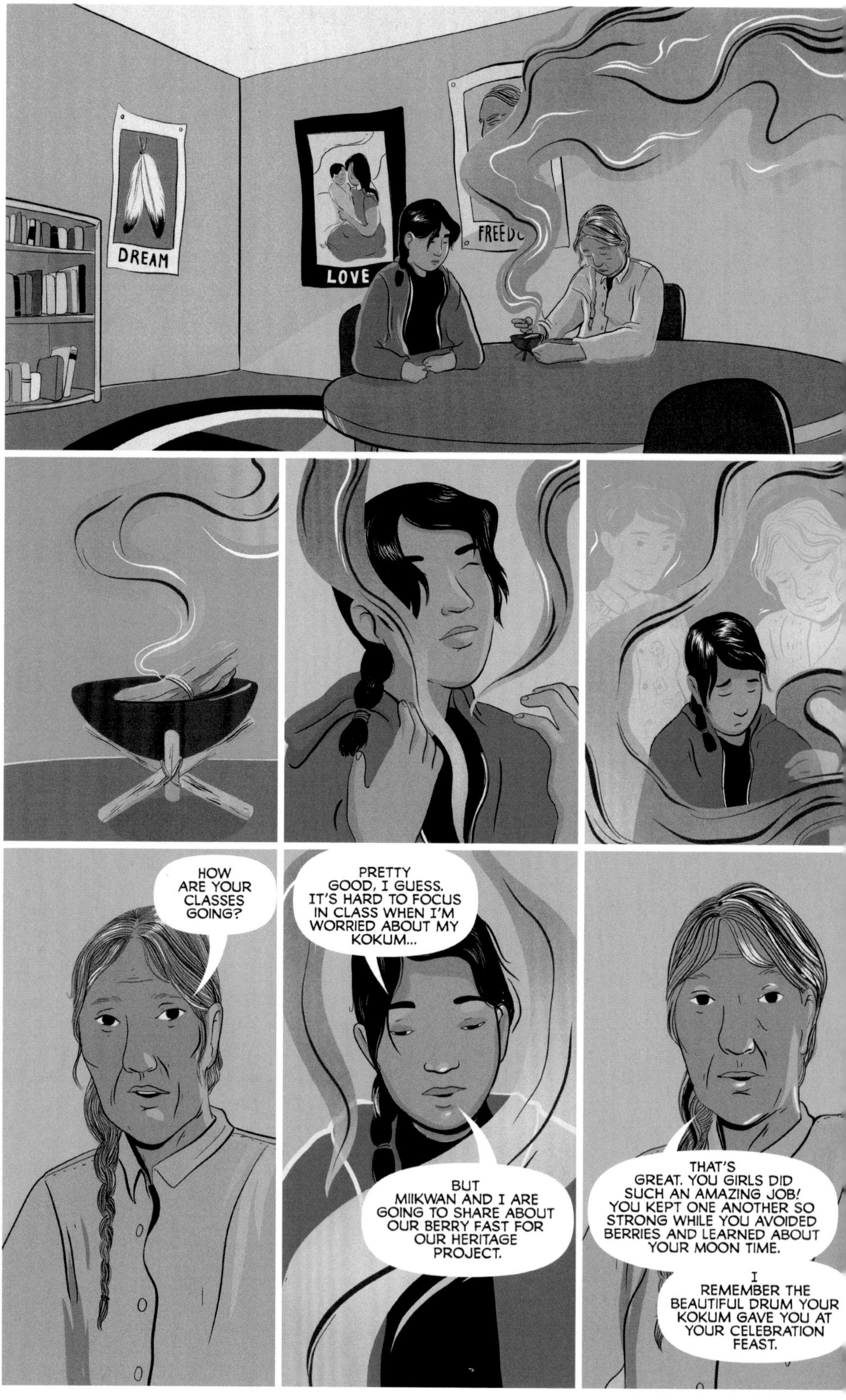
DREAM
LOVE
FREED
HOW ARE YOUR CLASSES GOING?
PRETTY GOOD, I GUESS. IT'S HARD TO FOCUS IN CLASS WHEN I'M WORRIED ABOUT MY KOKUM...
BUT MIIKWAN AND I ARE GOING TO SHARE ABOUT OUR BERRY FAST FOR OUR HERITAGE PROJECT.
THAT'S GREAT. YOU GIRLS DID SUCH AN AMAZING JOB! YOU KEPT ONE ANOTHER SO STRONG WHILE YOU AVOIDED BERRIES AND LEARNED ABOUT YOUR MOON TIME.
I REMEMBER THE BEAUTIFUL DRUM YOUR KOKUM GAVE YOU AT YOUR CELEBRATION FEAST.

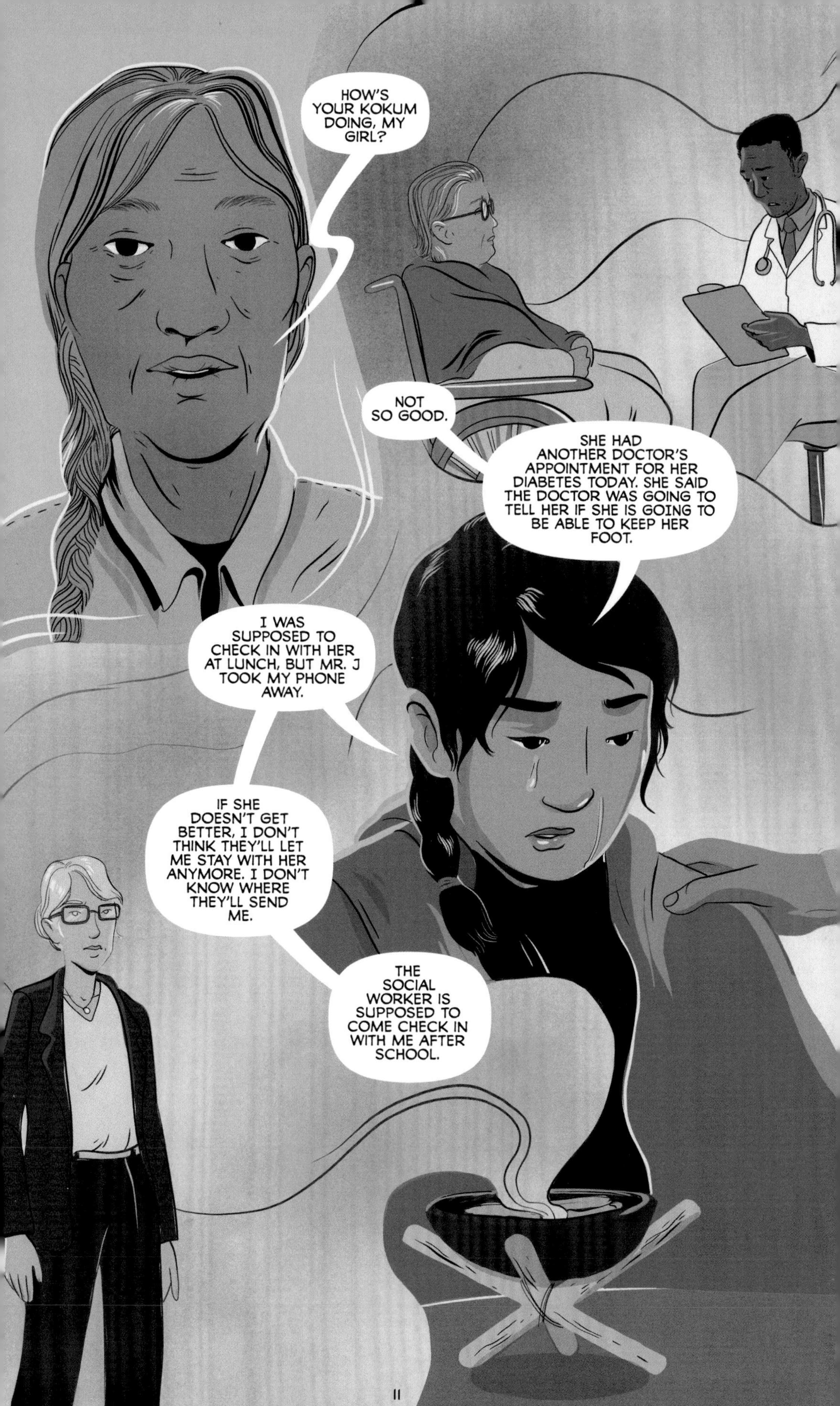
HOW'S YOUR KOKUM DOING, MY GIRL?
NOT SO GOOD.
SHE HAD ANOTHER DOCTOR'S APPOINTMENT FOR HER DIABETES TODAY. SHE SAID THE DOCTOR WAS GOING TO TELL HER IF SHE IS GOING TO BE ABLE TO KEEP HER FOOT.
I WAS SUPPOSED TO CHECK IN WITH HER AT LUNCH, BUT MR. J TOOK MY PHONE AWAY.
IF SHE DOESN'T GET BETTER, I DON'T THINK THEY'LL LET ME STAY WITH HER ANYMORE. I DON'T KNOW WHERE THEY'LL SEND ME.
THE SOCIAL WORKER IS SUPPOSED TO COME CHECK IN WITH ME AFTER SCHOOL.

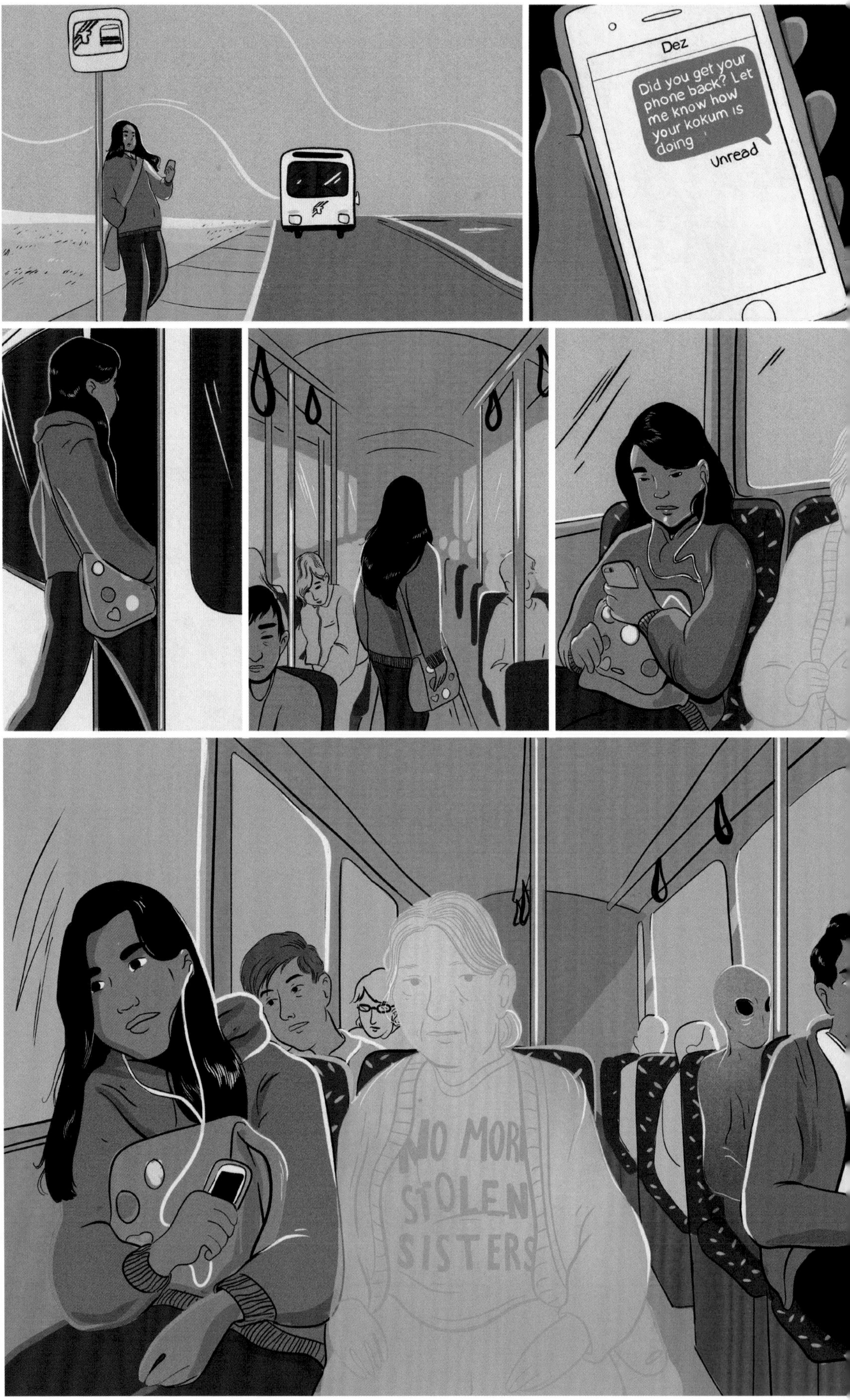
Dez
Did you get your phone back? Let me know how your kokum is doing
Unread
NO MORE STOLEN SISTERS

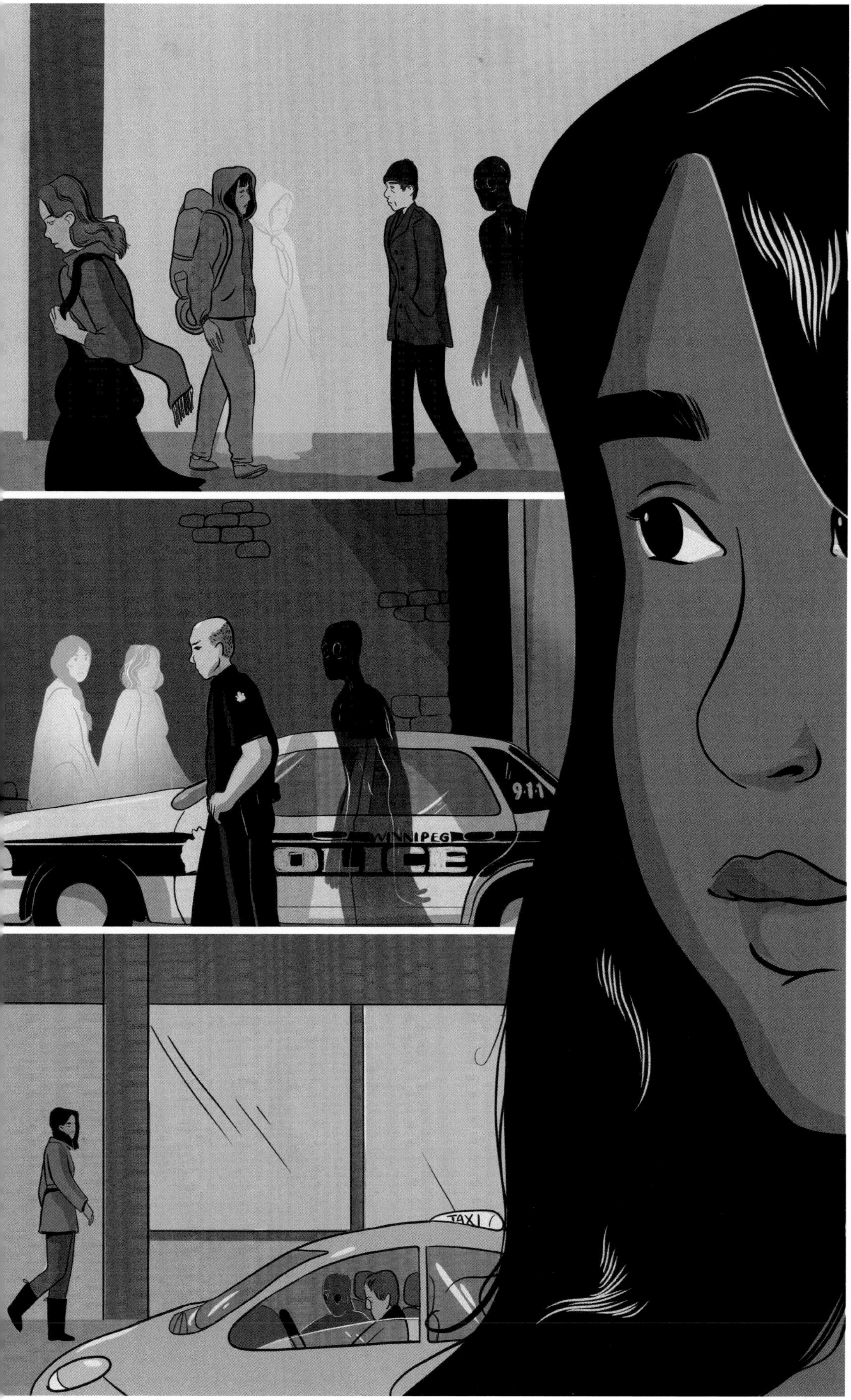
9·1·1
WINNIPEG
OLICE
TAXI

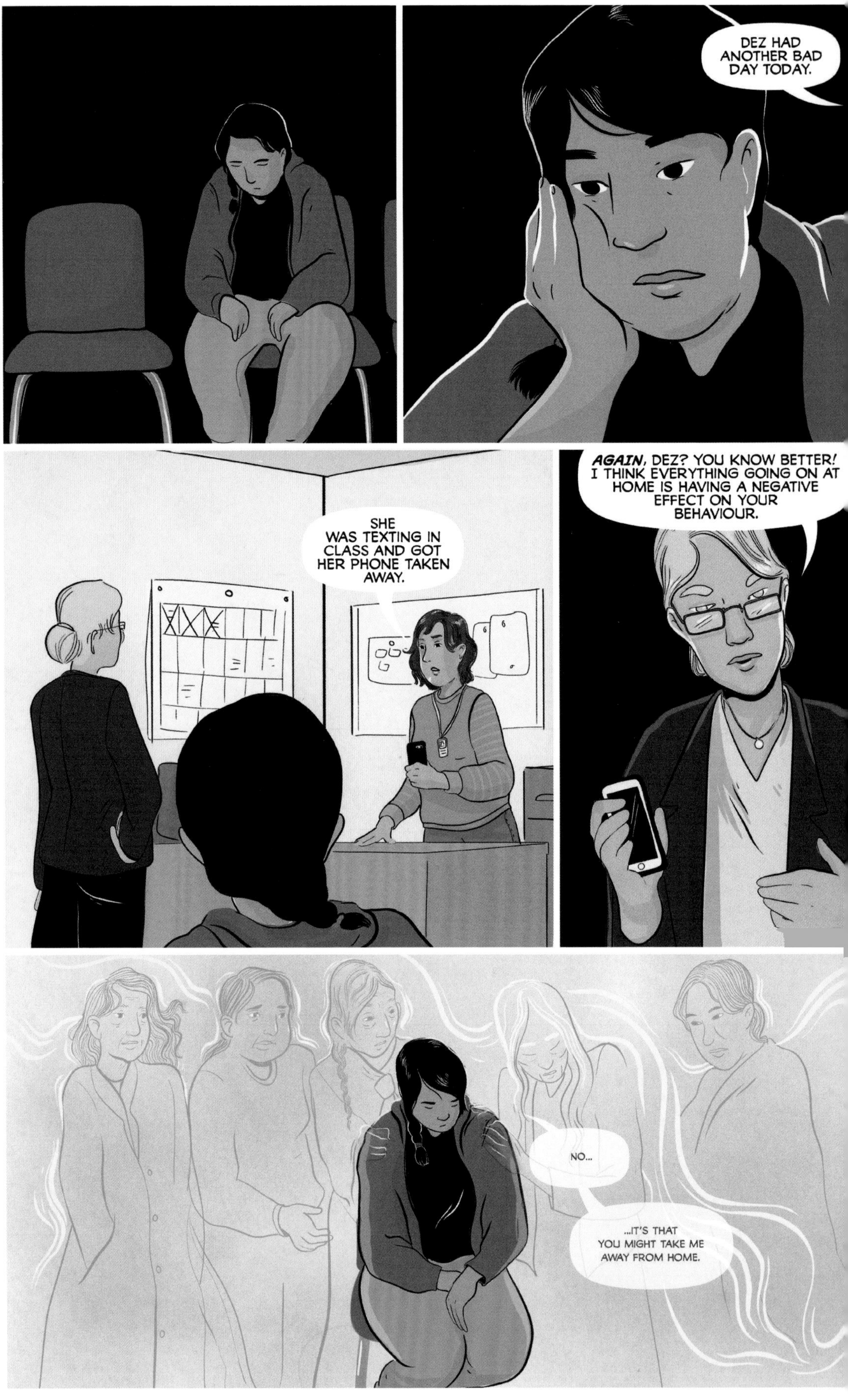
DEZ HAD ANOTHER BAD DAY TODAY.
SHE WAS TEXTING IN CLASS AND GOT HER PHONE TAKEN AWAY.
AGAIN, DEZ? YOU KNOW BETTER! I THINK EVERYTHING GOING ON AT HOME IS HAVING A NEGATIVE EFFECT ON YOUR BEHAVIOUR.
NO...
...IT'S THAT YOU MIGHT TAKE ME AWAY FROM HOME.

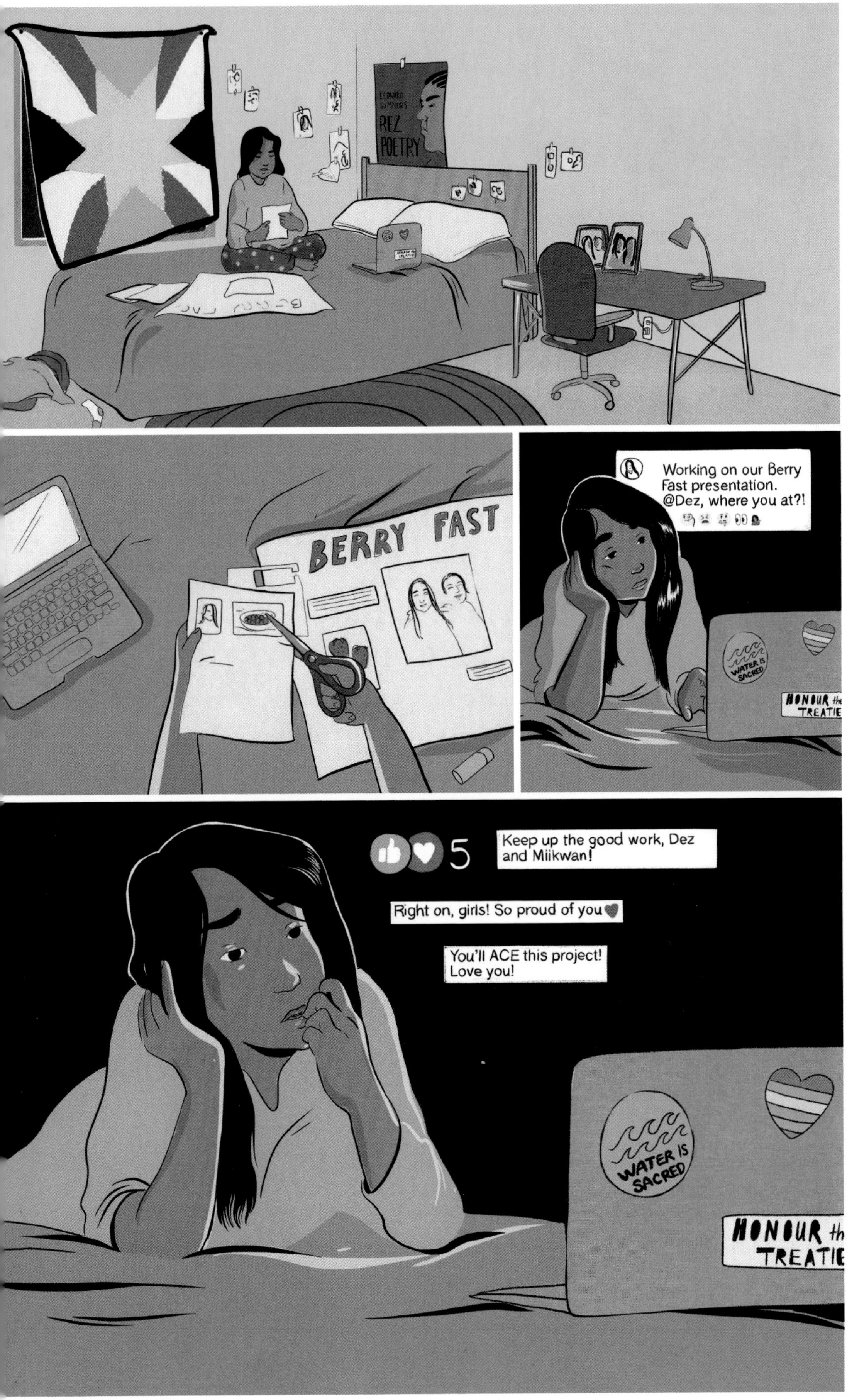
REZ POETRY
BERRY FAST
Working on our Berry Fast presentation. @Dez, where you at?!
WATER IS SACRED
HONOUR the TREATIE
5
Keep up the good work, Dez and Miikwan!
Right on, girls! So proud of you
You'll ACE this project! Love you!
WATER IS SACRED
HONOUR th TREATIE

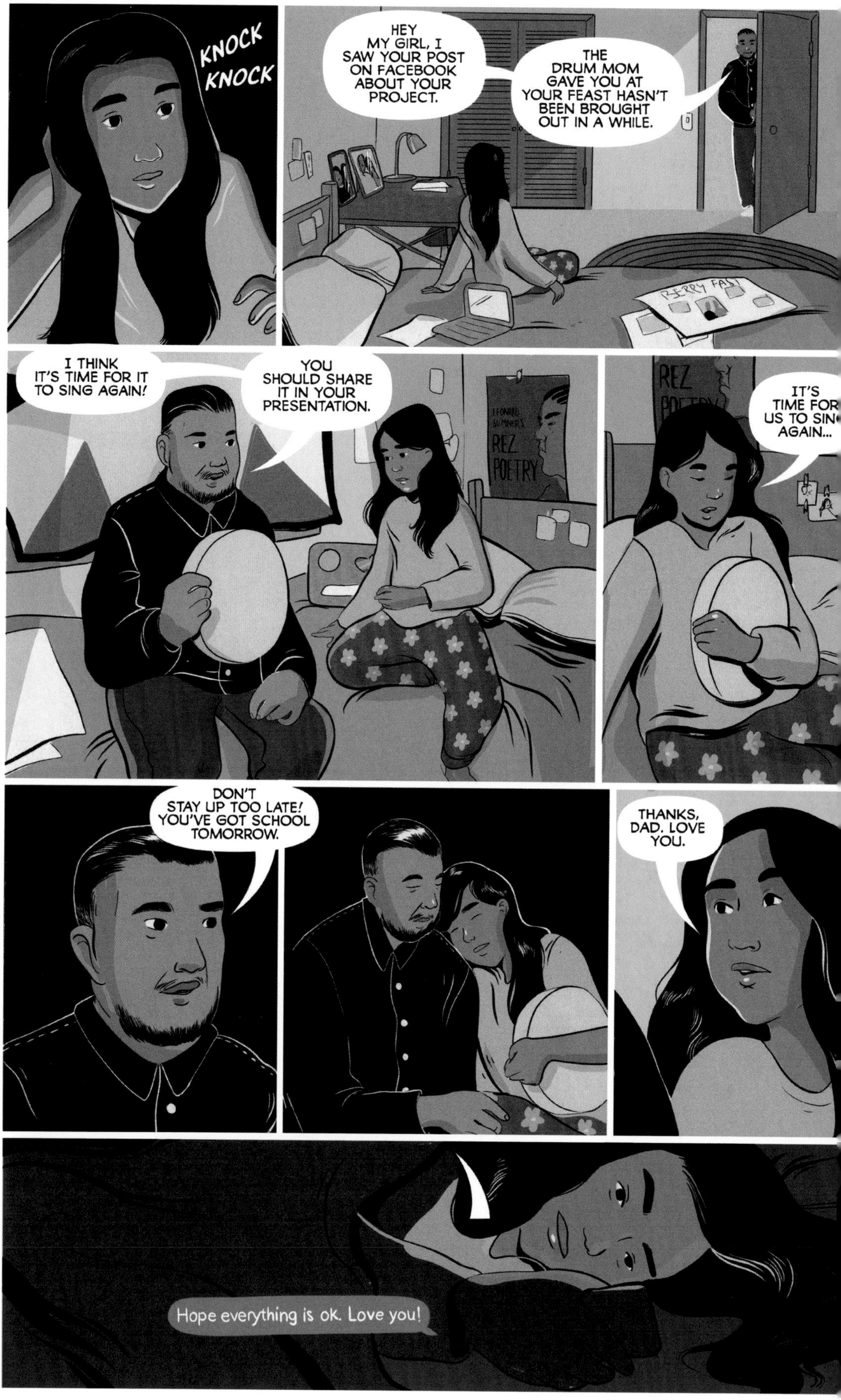
KNOCK KNOCK
HEY MY GIRL, I SAW YOUR POST ON FACEBOOK ABOUT YOUR PROJECT.
THE DRUM MOM GAVE YOU AT YOUR FEAST HASN'T BEEN BROUGHT OUT IN A WHILE.
BERRY FAST
I THINK IT'S TIME FOR IT TO SING AGAIN!
YOU SHOULD SHARE IT IN YOUR PRESENTATION.
LEONARD SUMNER'S REZ POETRY
IT'S TIME FOR US TO SIN AGAIN...
DON'T STAY UP TOO LATE! YOU'VE GOT SCHOOL TOMORROW.
THANKS, DAD. LOVE YOU.
Hope everything is ok. Love you!

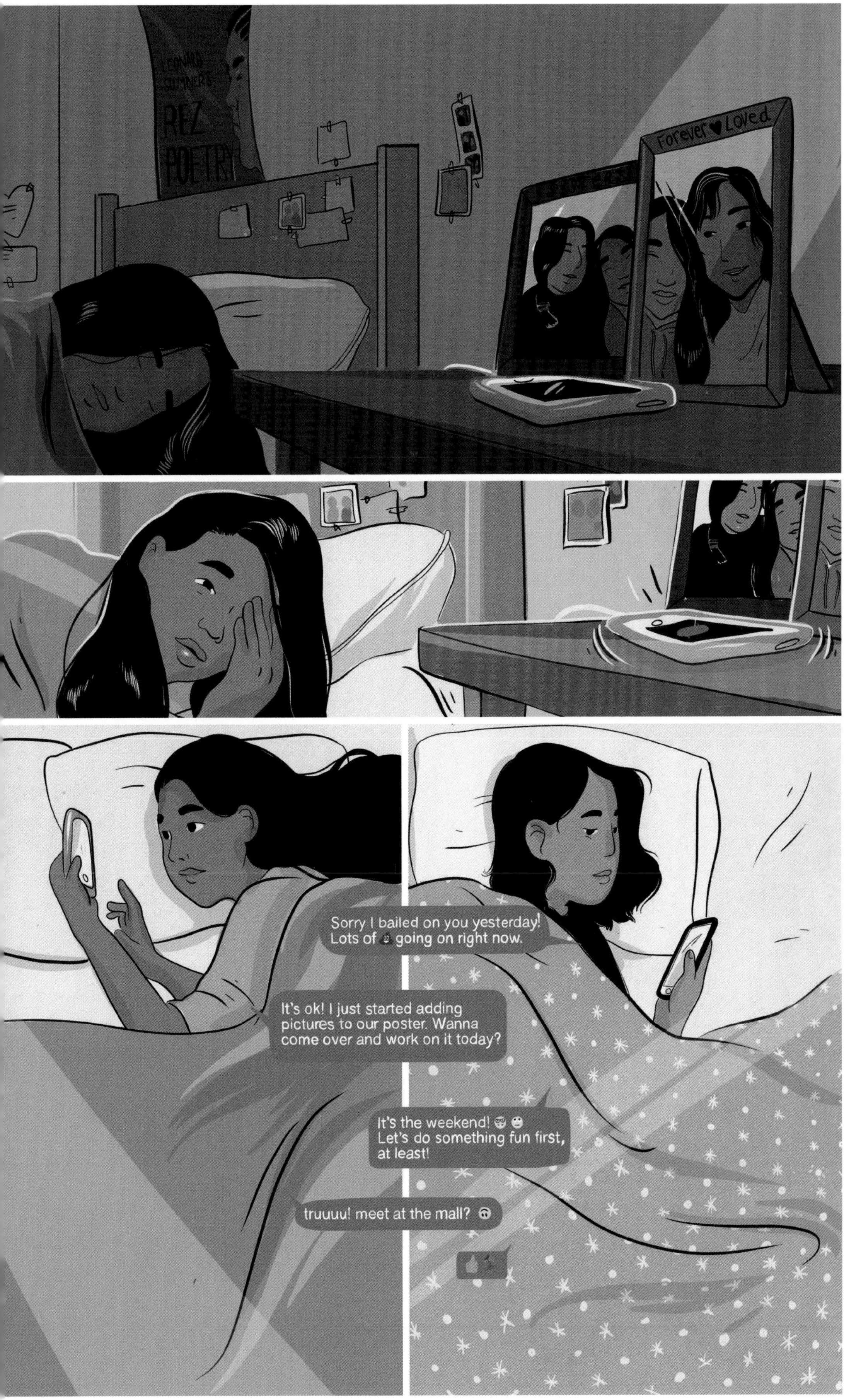
LEONARD SUMNER'S
REZ POETRY
Forever ♥ Loved
Sorry I bailed on you yesterday! Lots of 💩 going on right now.
It's ok! I just started adding pictures to our poster. Wanna come over and work on it today?
It's the weekend! 🤓 🙂 Let's do something fun first, at least!
truuuu! meet at the mall? 🙃

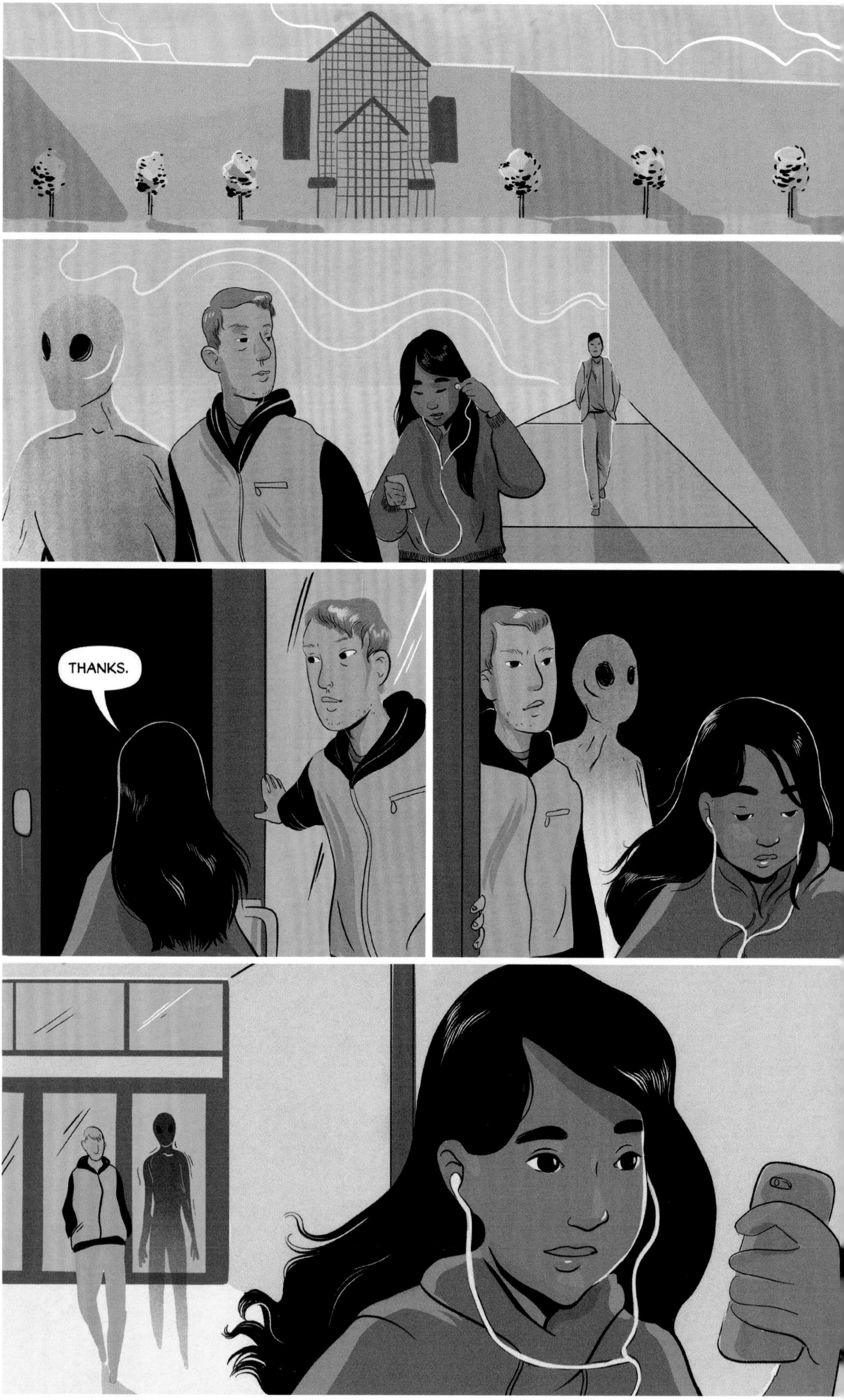
THANKS.

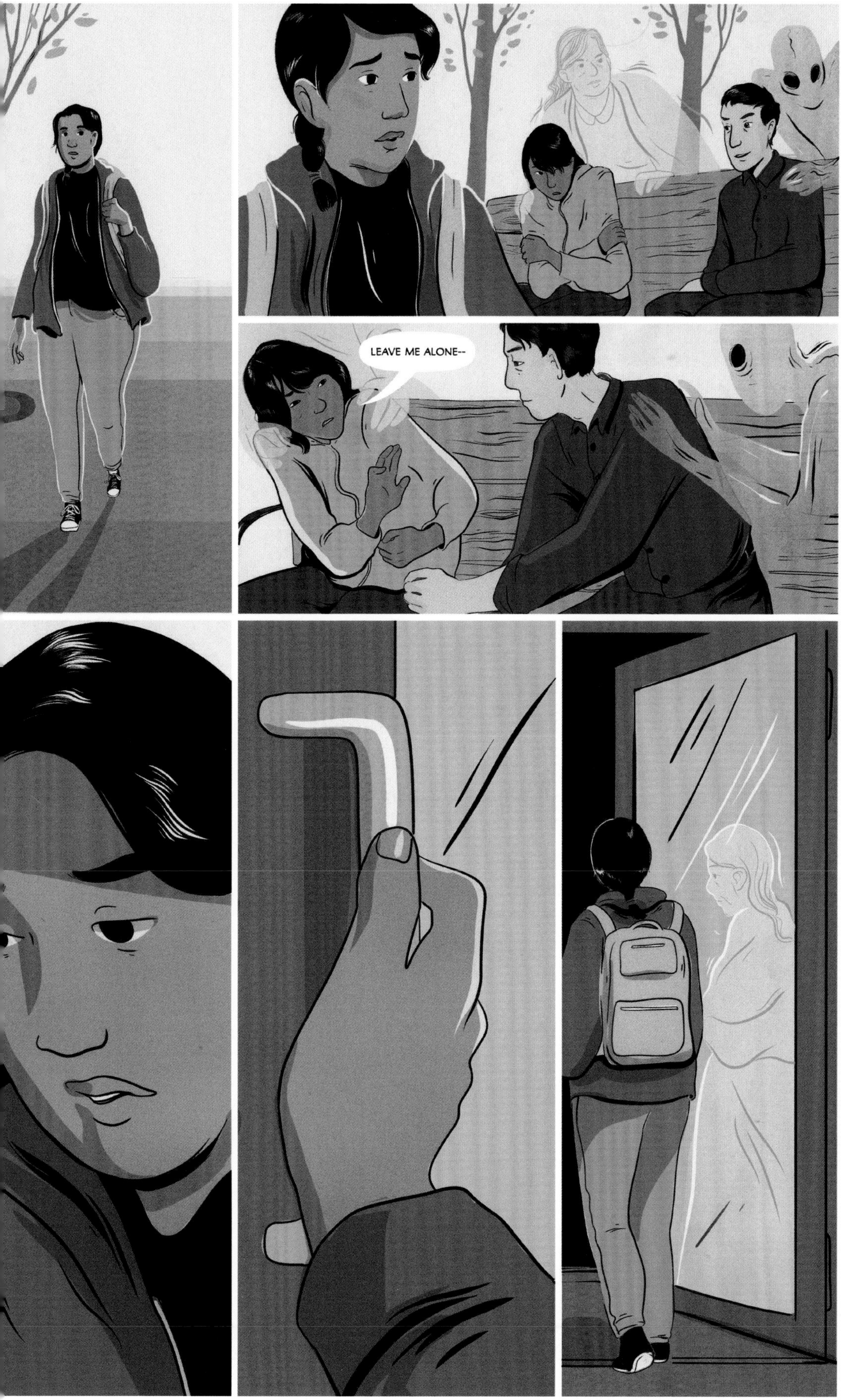
LEAVE ME ALONE--

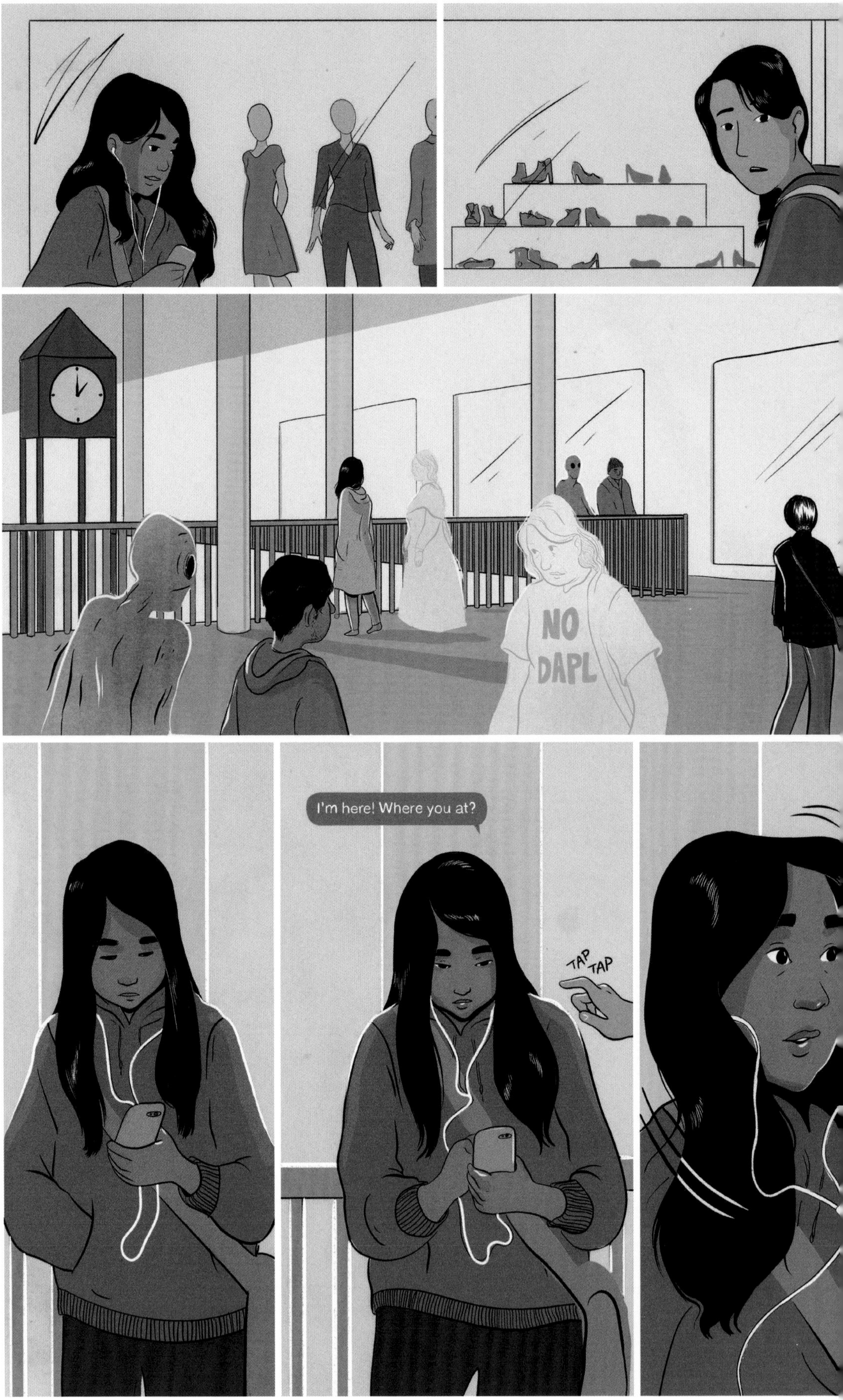
NO DAPL
I'm here! Where you at?
TAP TAP

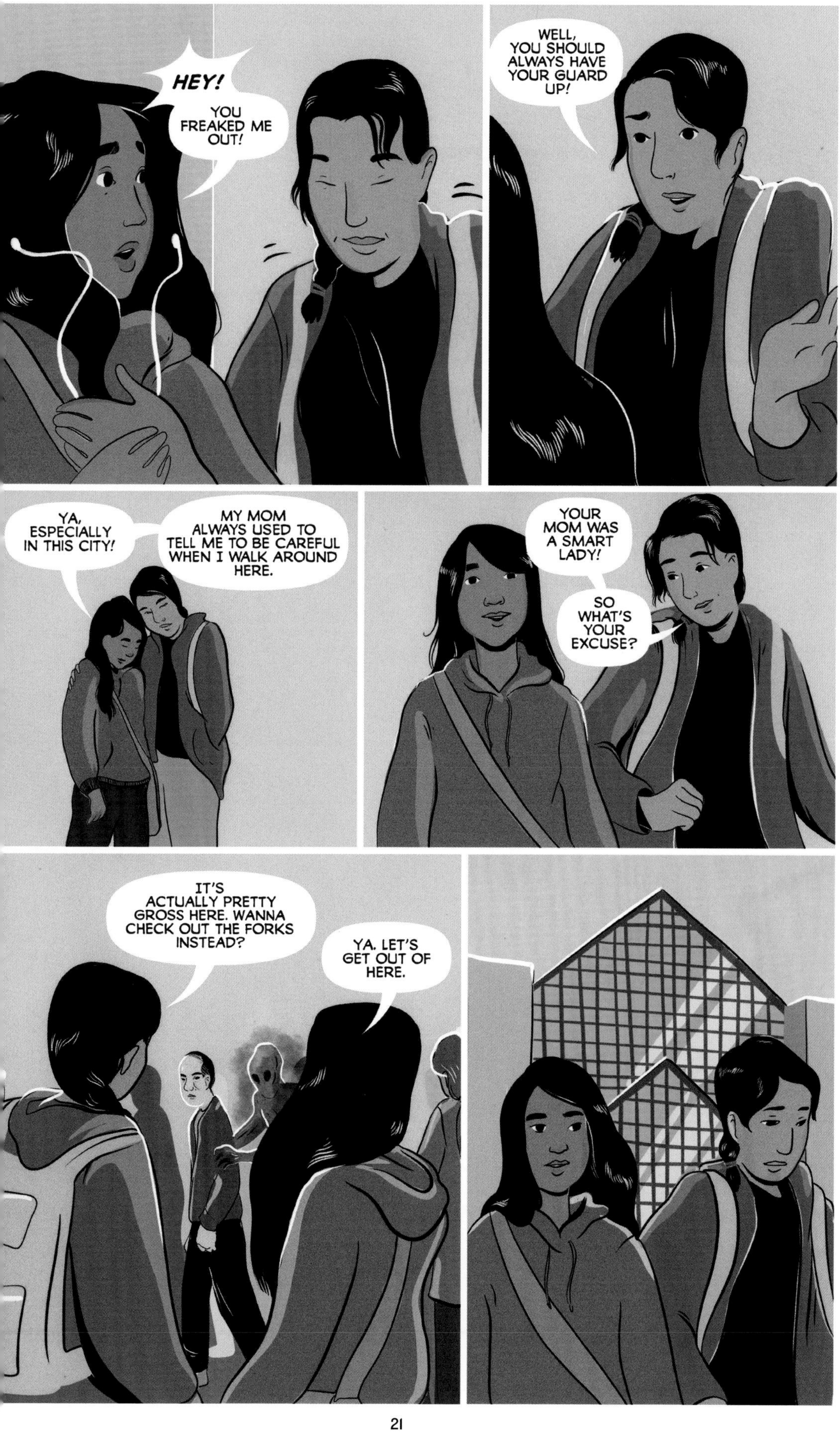
HEY!
YOU FREAKED ME OUT!
WELL, YOU SHOULD ALWAYS HAVE YOUR GUARD UP!
MY MOM ALWAYS USED TO TELL ME TO BE CAREFUL WHEN I WALK AROUND HERE.
YA, ESPECIALLY IN THIS CITY!
YOUR MOM WAS A SMART LADY!
SO WHAT'S YOUR EXCUSE?
IT'S ACTUALLY PRETTY GROSS HERE. WANNA CHECK OUT THE FORKS INSTEAD?
YA. LET'S GET OUT OF HERE.

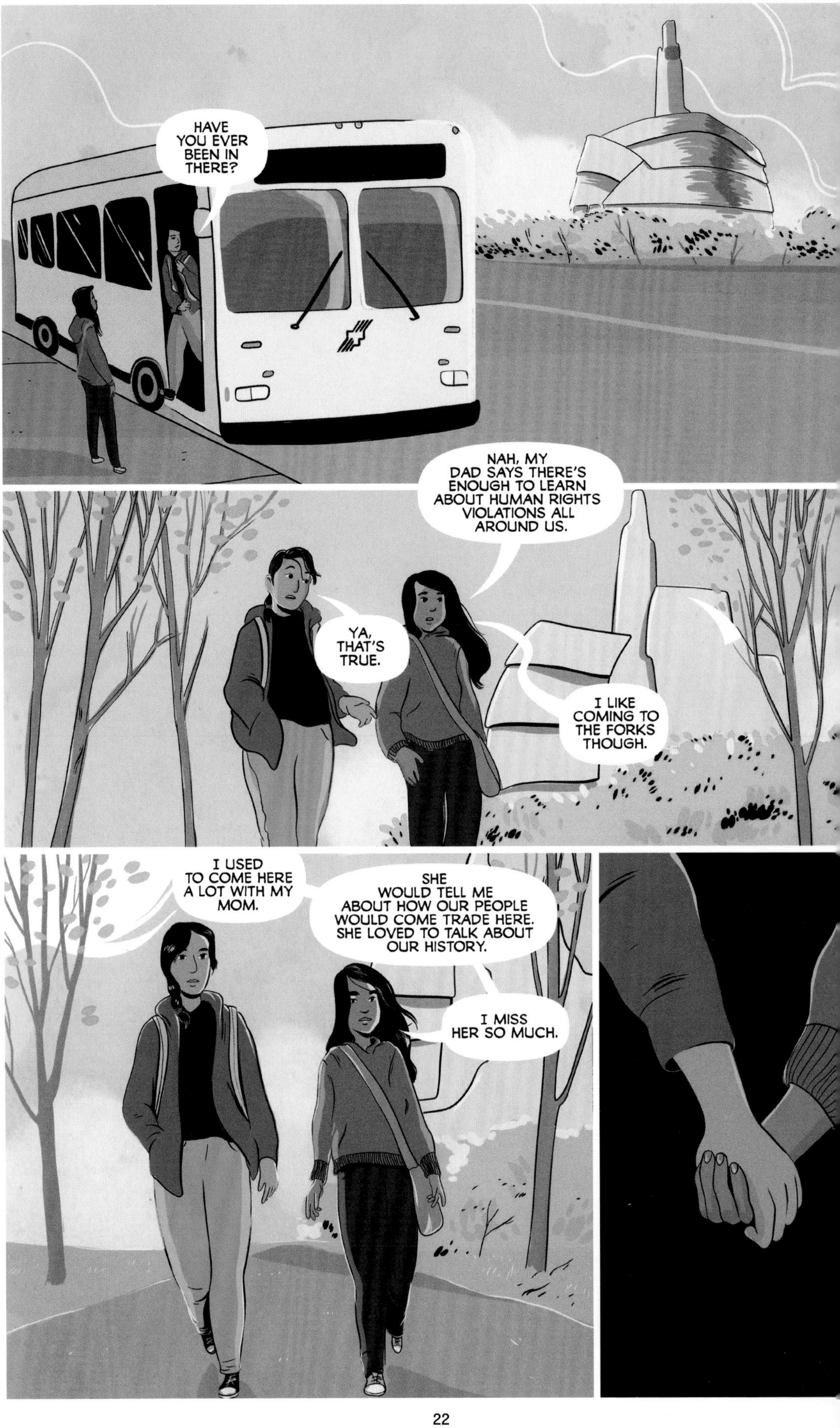
HAVE YOU EVER BEEN IN THERE?
NAH, MY DAD SAYS THERE'S ENOUGH TO LEARN ABOUT HUMAN RIGHTS VIOLATIONS ALL AROUND US.
YA, THAT'S TRUE.
I LIKE COMING TO THE FORKS THOUGH.
I USED TO COME HERE A LOT WITH MY MOM.
SHE WOULD TELL ME ABOUT HOW OUR PEOPLE WOULD COME TRADE HERE. SHE LOVED TO TALK ABOUT OUR HISTORY.
I MISS HER SO MUCH.

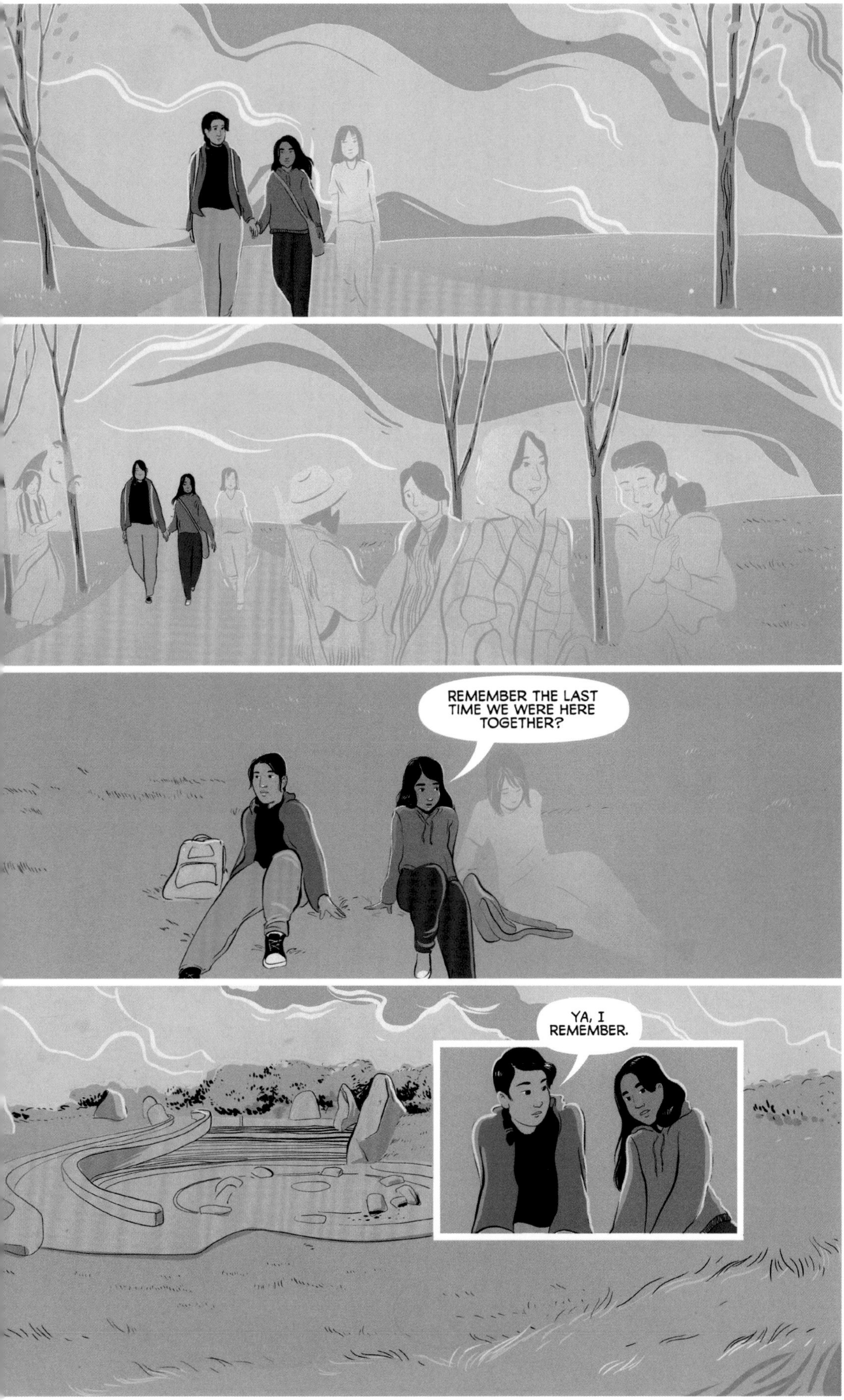
REMEMBER THE LAST TIME WE WERE HERE TOGETHER?
YA, I REMEMBER.

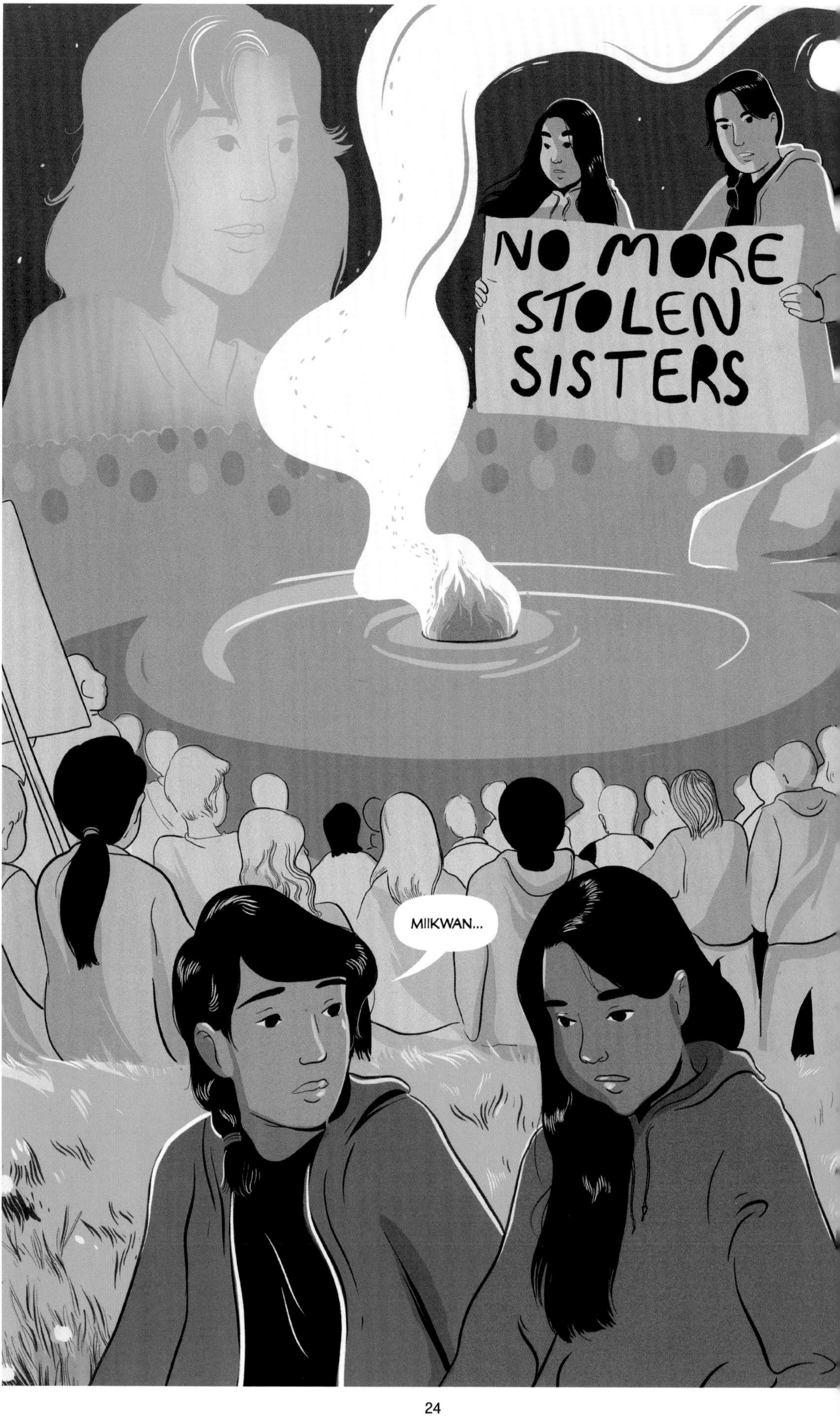
NO MORE STOLEN SISTERS
MIIKWAN...

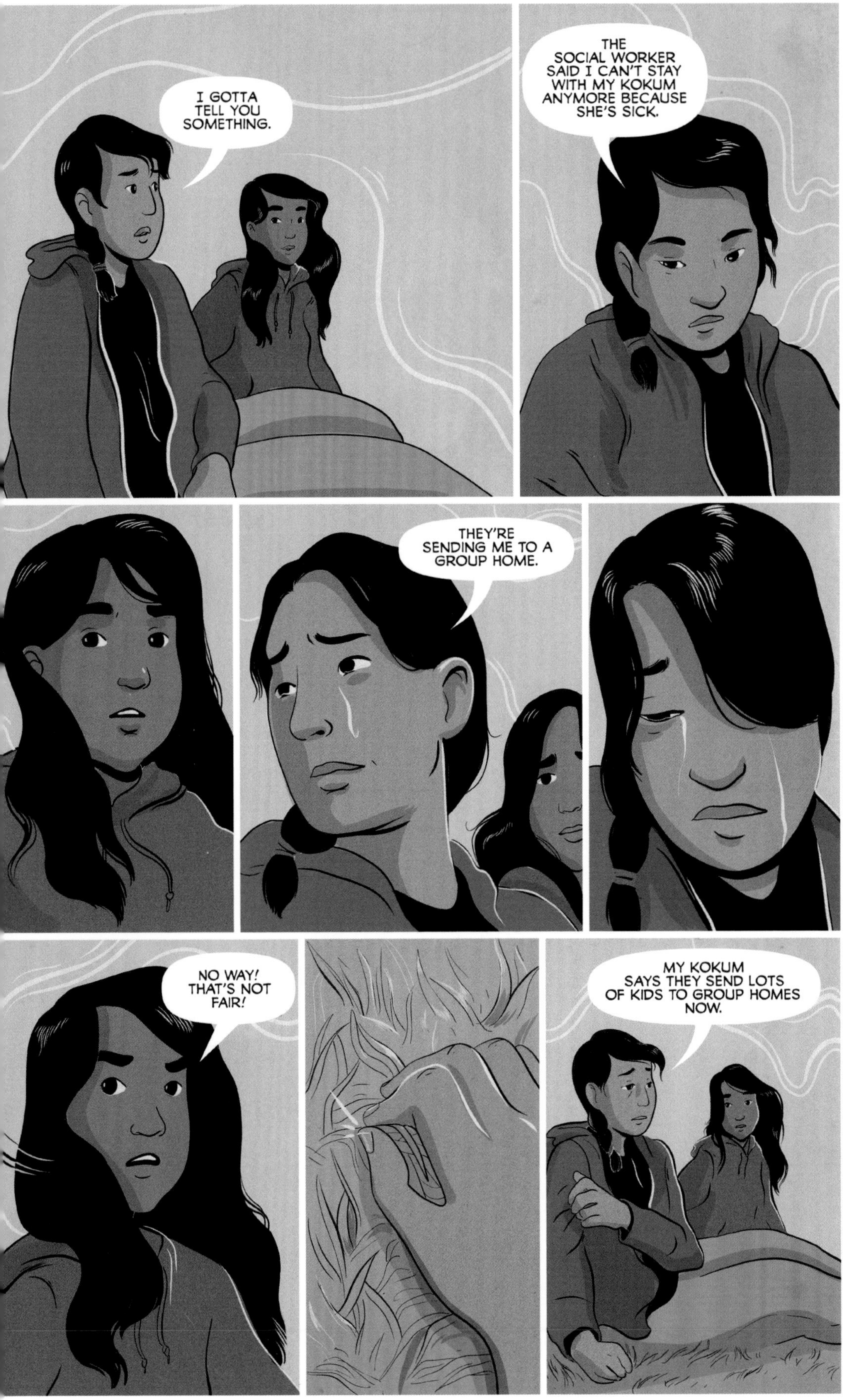
I GOTTA TELL YOU SOMETHING.
THE SOCIAL WORKER SAID I CAN'T STAY WITH MY KOKUM ANYMORE BECAUSE SHE'S SICK.
THEY'RE SENDING ME TO A GROUP HOME.
NO WAY! THAT'S NOT FAIR!
MY KOKUM SAYS THEY SEND LOTS OF KIDS TO GROUP HOMES NOW.

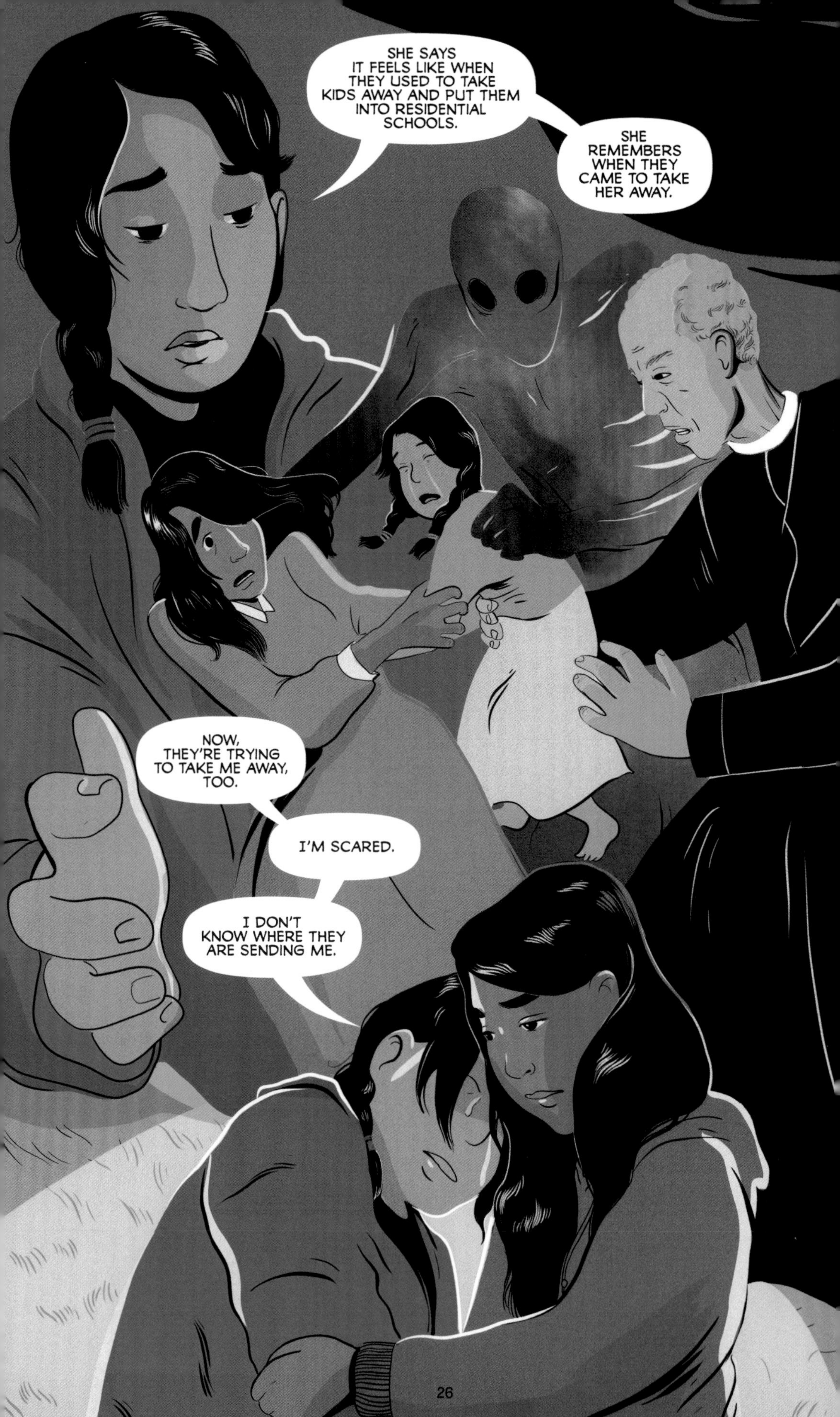
SHE SAYS IT FEELS LIKE WHEN THEY USED TO TAKE KIDS AWAY AND PUT THEM INTO RESIDENTIAL SCHOOLS.
SHE REMEMBERS WHEN THEY CAME TO TAKE HER AWAY.
NOW, THEY'RE TRYING TO TAKE ME AWAY, TOO.
I'M SCARED.
I DON'T KNOW WHERE THEY ARE SENDING ME.

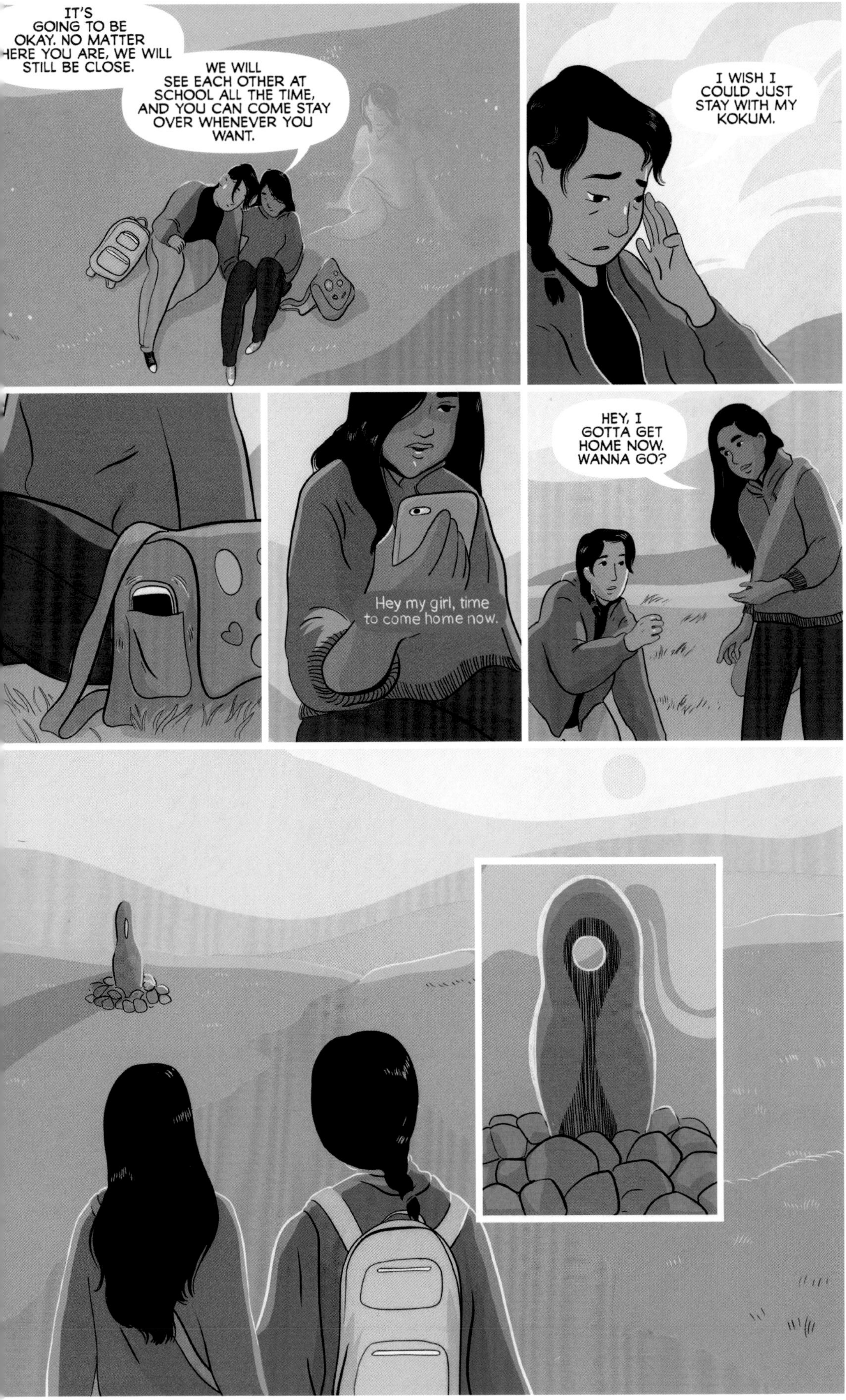
IT'S GOING TO BE OKAY. NO MATTER HERE YOU ARE, WE WILL STILL BE CLOSE.
WE WILL SEE EACH OTHER AT SCHOOL ALL THE TIME, AND YOU CAN COME STAY OVER WHENEVER YOU WANT.
I WISH I COULD JUST STAY WITH MY KOKUM.
Hey my girl, time to come home now.
HEY, I GOTTA GET HOME NOW. WANNA GO?

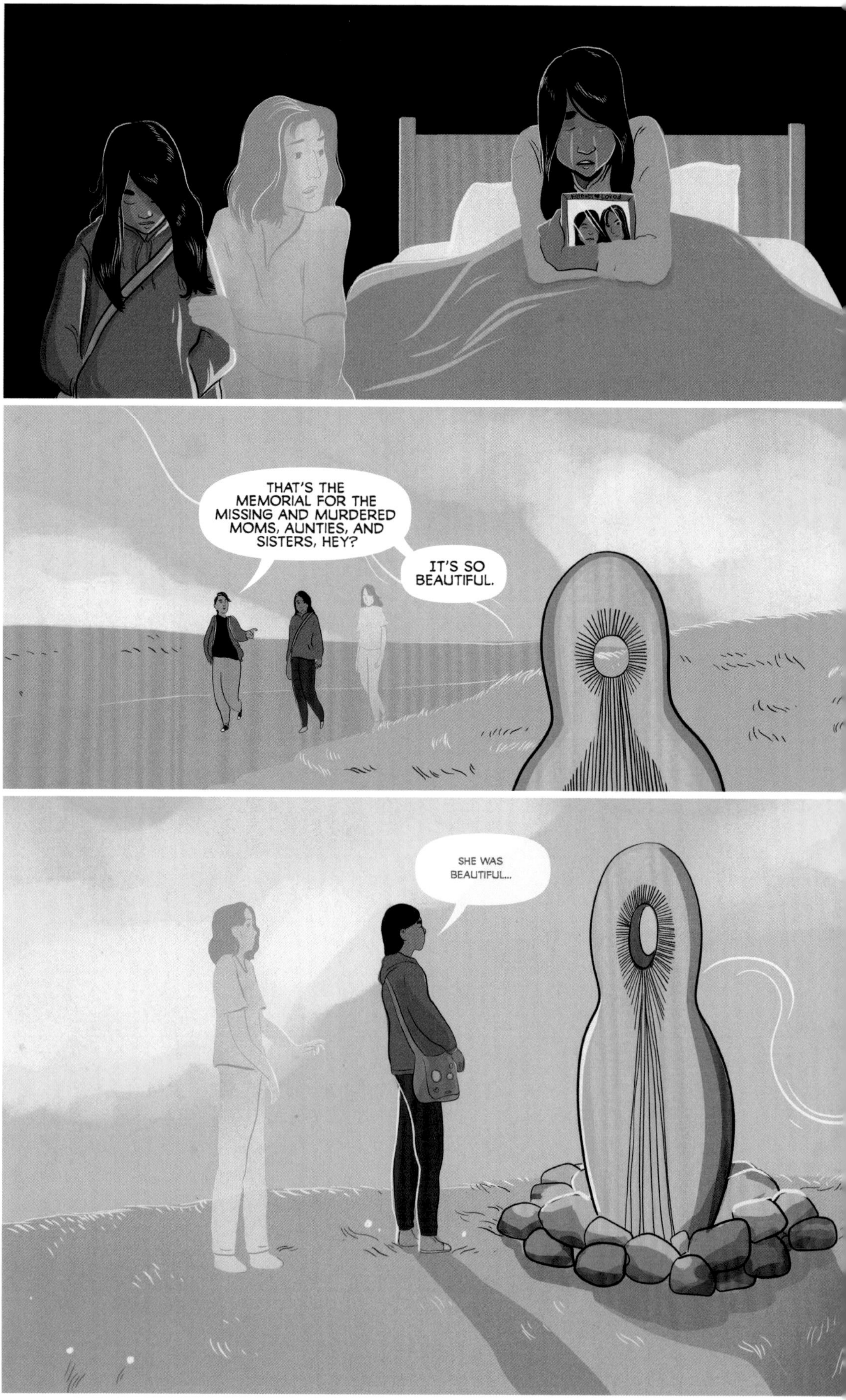
THAT'S THE MEMORIAL FOR THE MISSING AND MURDERED MOMS, AUNTIES, AND SISTERS, HEY?
IT'S SO BEAUTIFUL.
SHE WAS BEAUTIFUL...

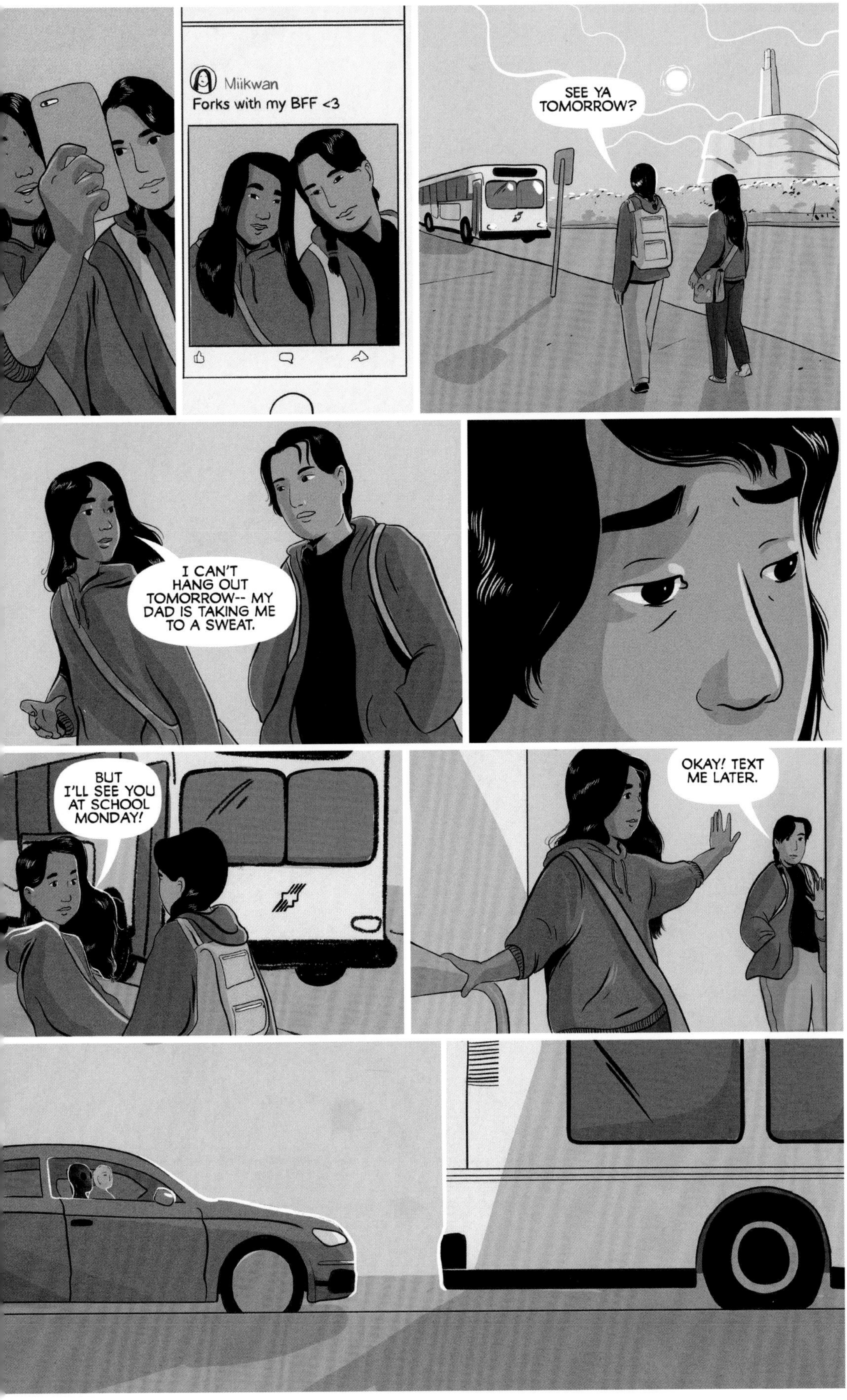
Miikwan
Forks with my BFF <3
SEE YA TOMORROW?
I CAN'T HANG OUT TOMORROW-- MY DAD IS TAKING ME TO A SWEAT.
BUT I'LL SEE YOU AT SCHOOL MONDAY!
OKAY! TEXT ME LATER.

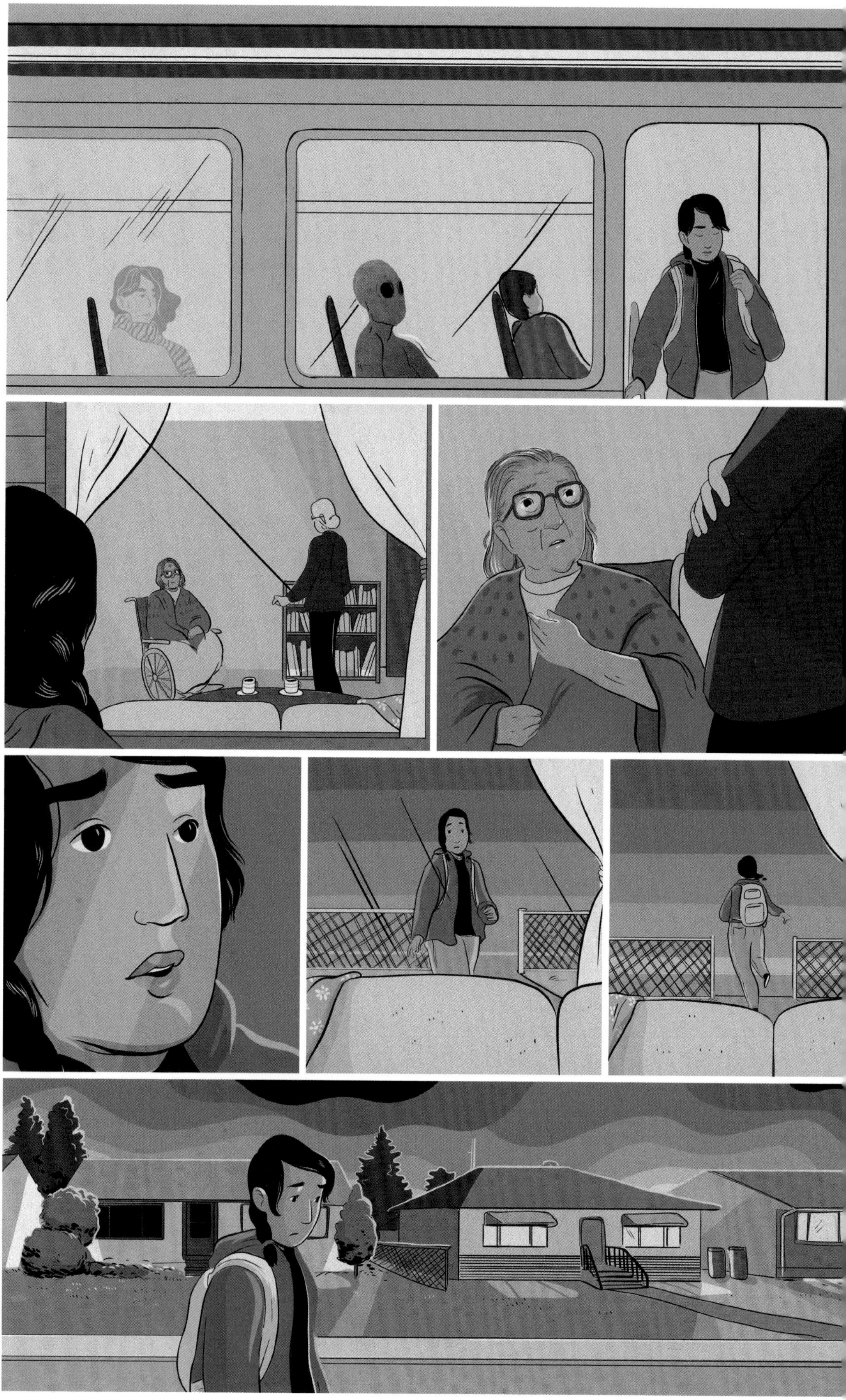

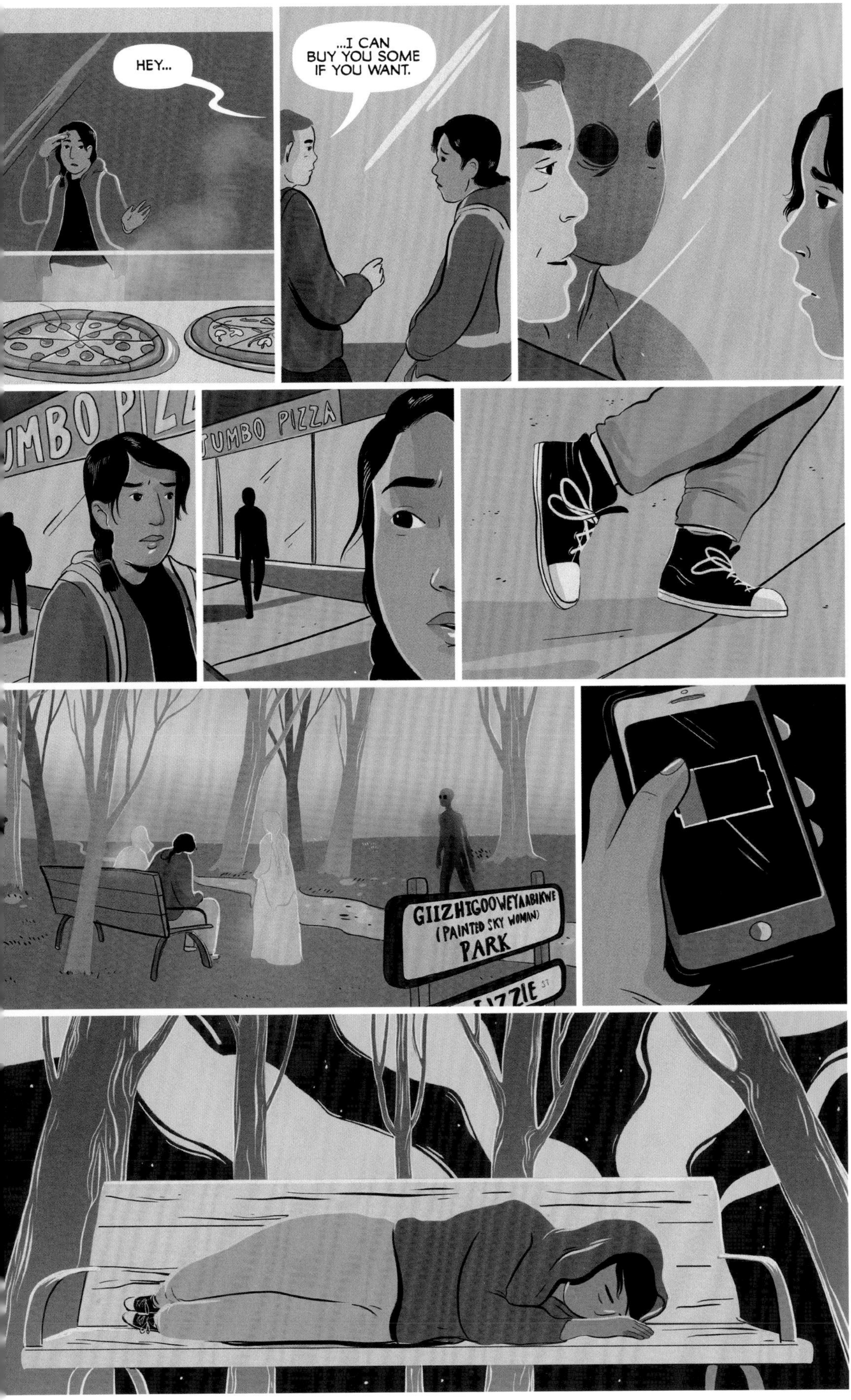
HEY...
...I CAN BUY YOU SOME IF YOU WANT.
JUMBO PIZZA
JUMBO PIZZA
GIIZHIGOOWEYAABIKWE (PAINTED SKY WOMAN) PARK
LIZZIE ST

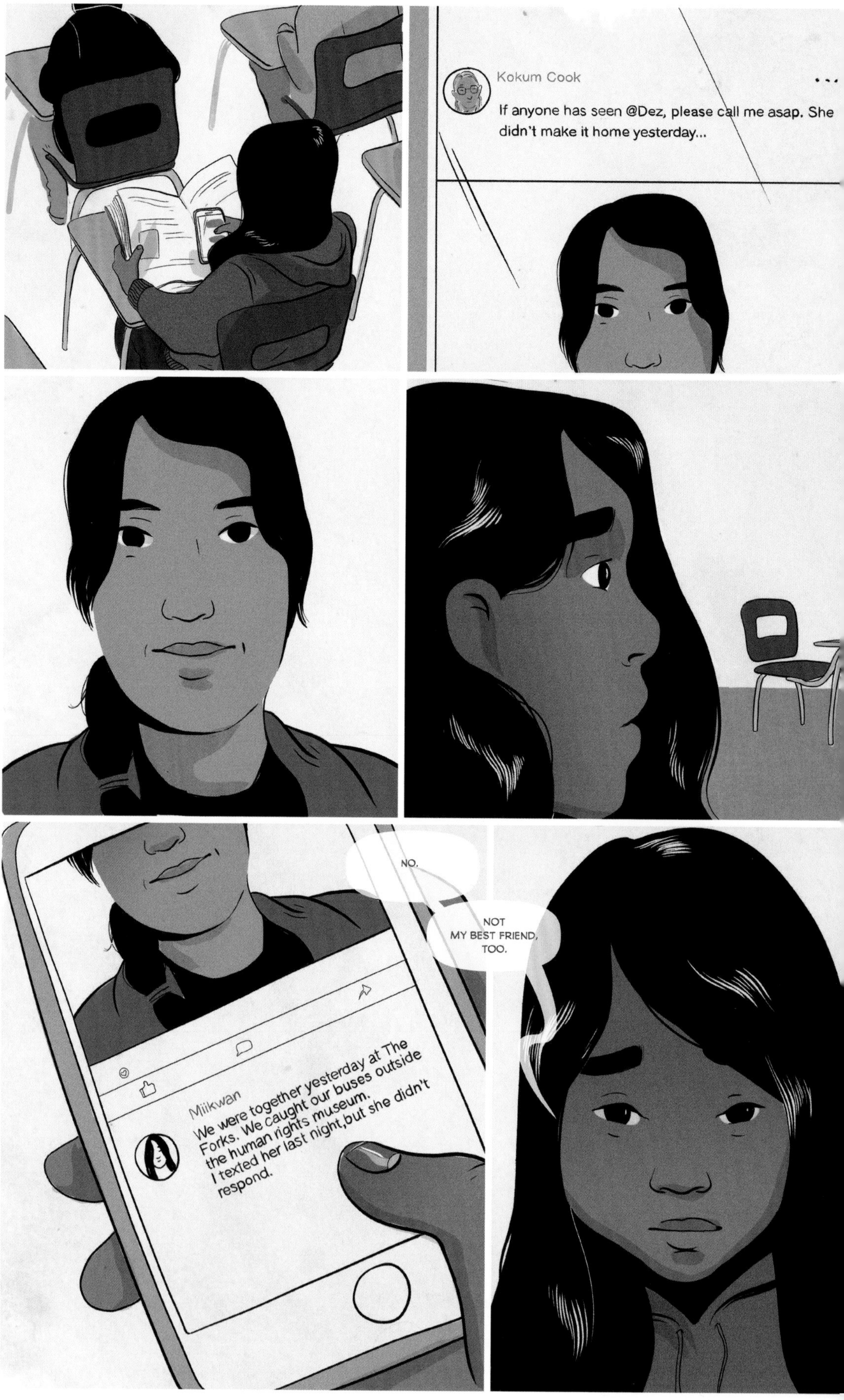
Kokum Cook
If anyone has seen @Dez, please call me asap. She didn't make it home yesterday...
NO.
NOT MY BEST FRIEND, TOO.
Miikwan
We were together yesterday at The Forks. We caught our buses outside the human rights museum. I texted her last night,but she didn't respond.

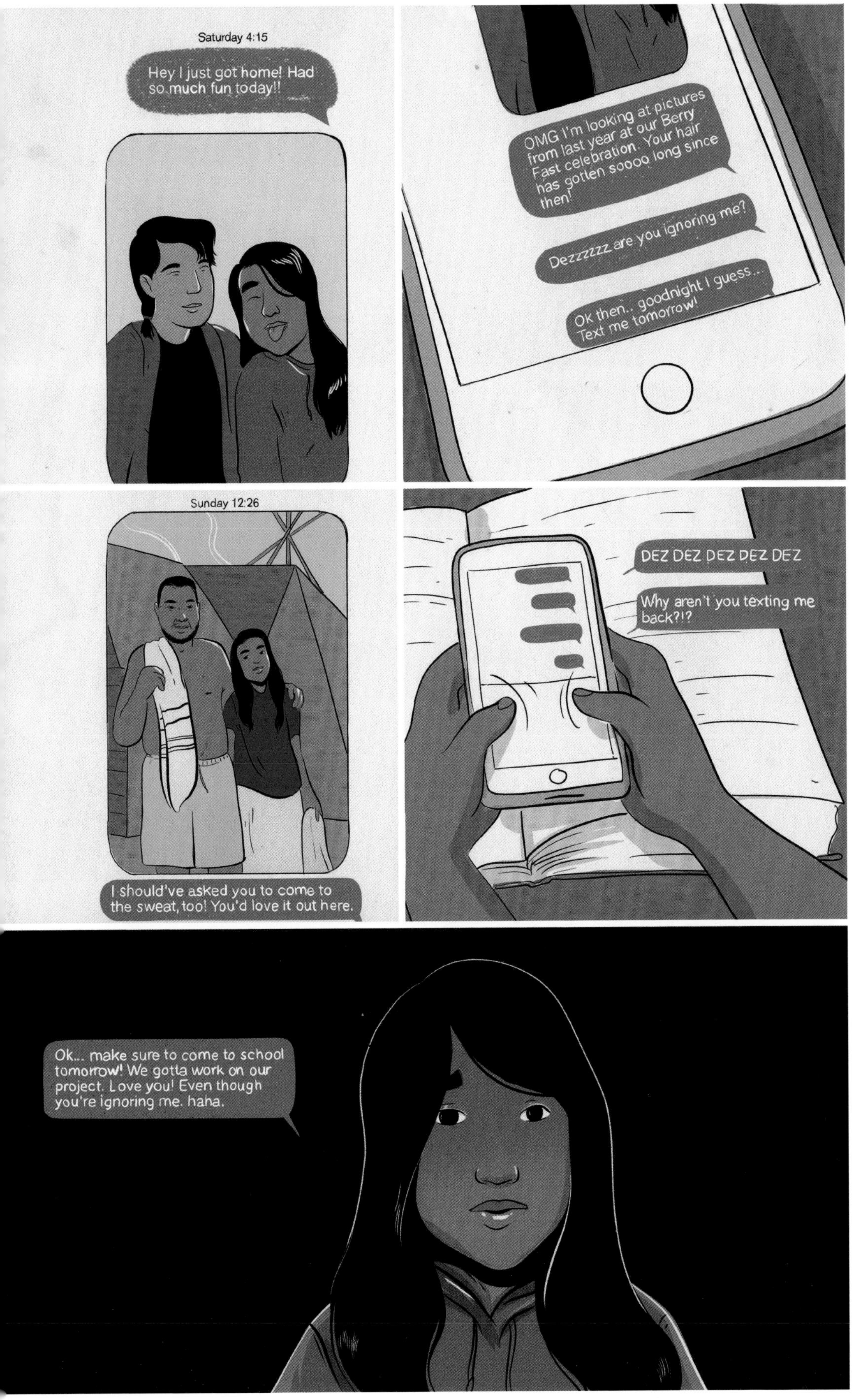
Saturday 4:15
Hey I just got home! Had so much fun today!!
OMG I'm looking at pictures from last year at our Berry Fast celebration. Your hair has gotten soooo long since then!
Dezzzzzz are you ignoring me?
Ok then.. goodnight I guess...
Text me tomorrow!
Sunday 12:26
I should've asked you to come to the sweat, too! You'd love it out here.
DEZ DEZ DEZ DEZ DEZ
Why aren't you texting me back?!?
Ok... make sure to come to school tomorrow! We gotta work on our project. Love you! Even though you're ignoring me. haha.

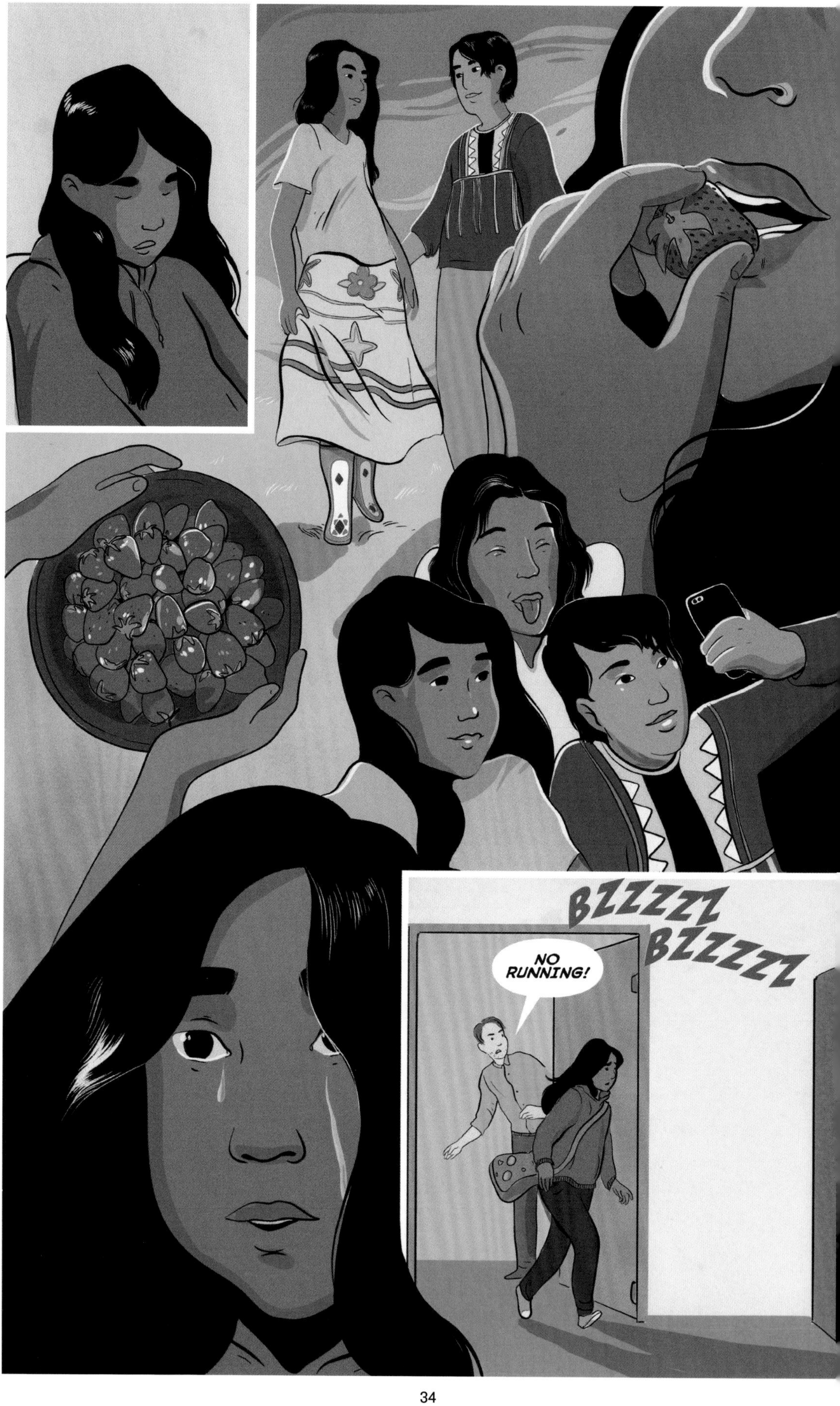
BZZZZZ
BZZZZZ
NO RUNNING!

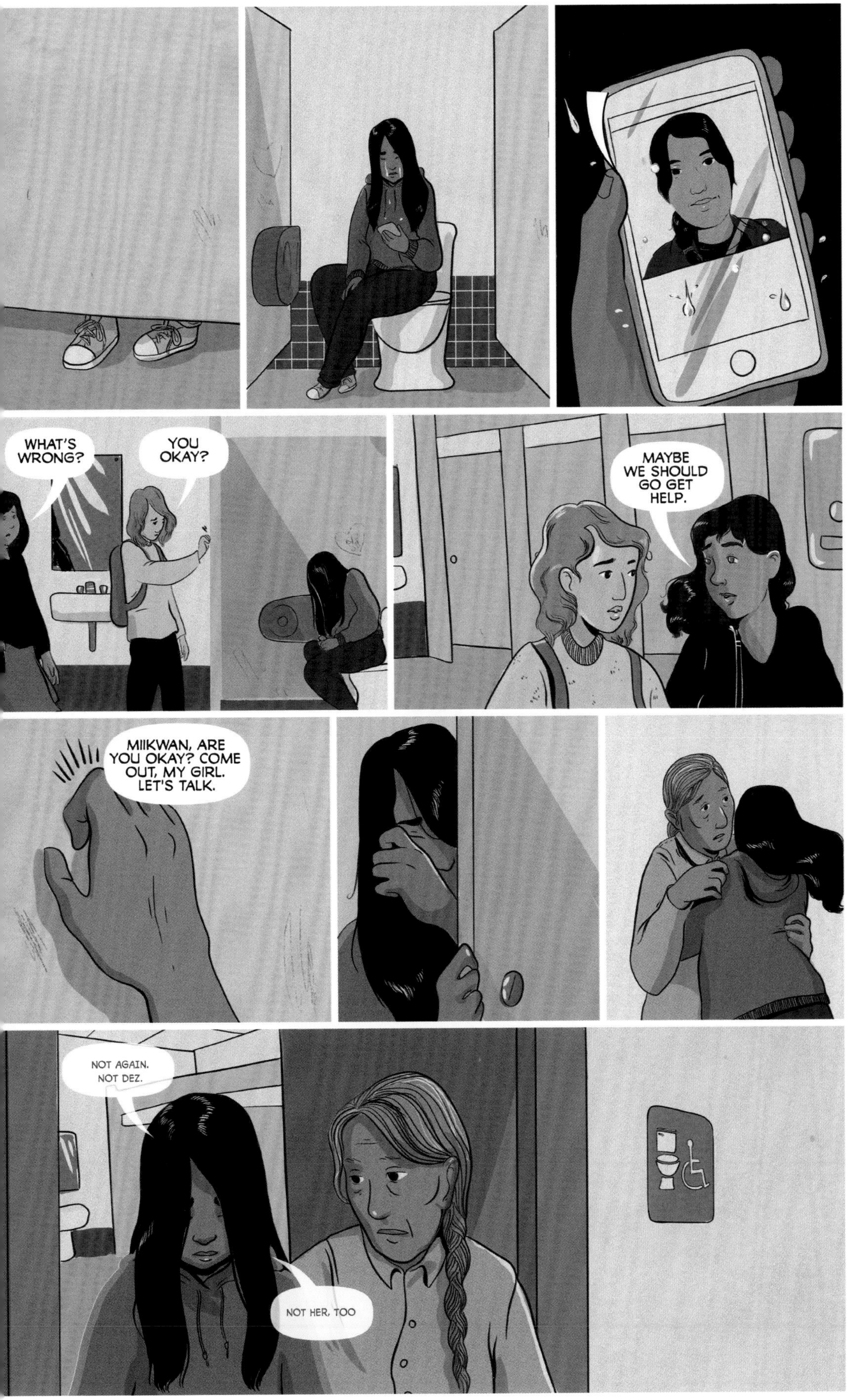
WHAT'S WRONG?
YOU OKAY?
MAYBE WE SHOULD GO GET HELP.
MIIKWAN, ARE YOU OKAY? COME OUT, MY GIRL. LET'S TALK.
NOT AGAIN. NOT DEZ.
NOT HER, TOO

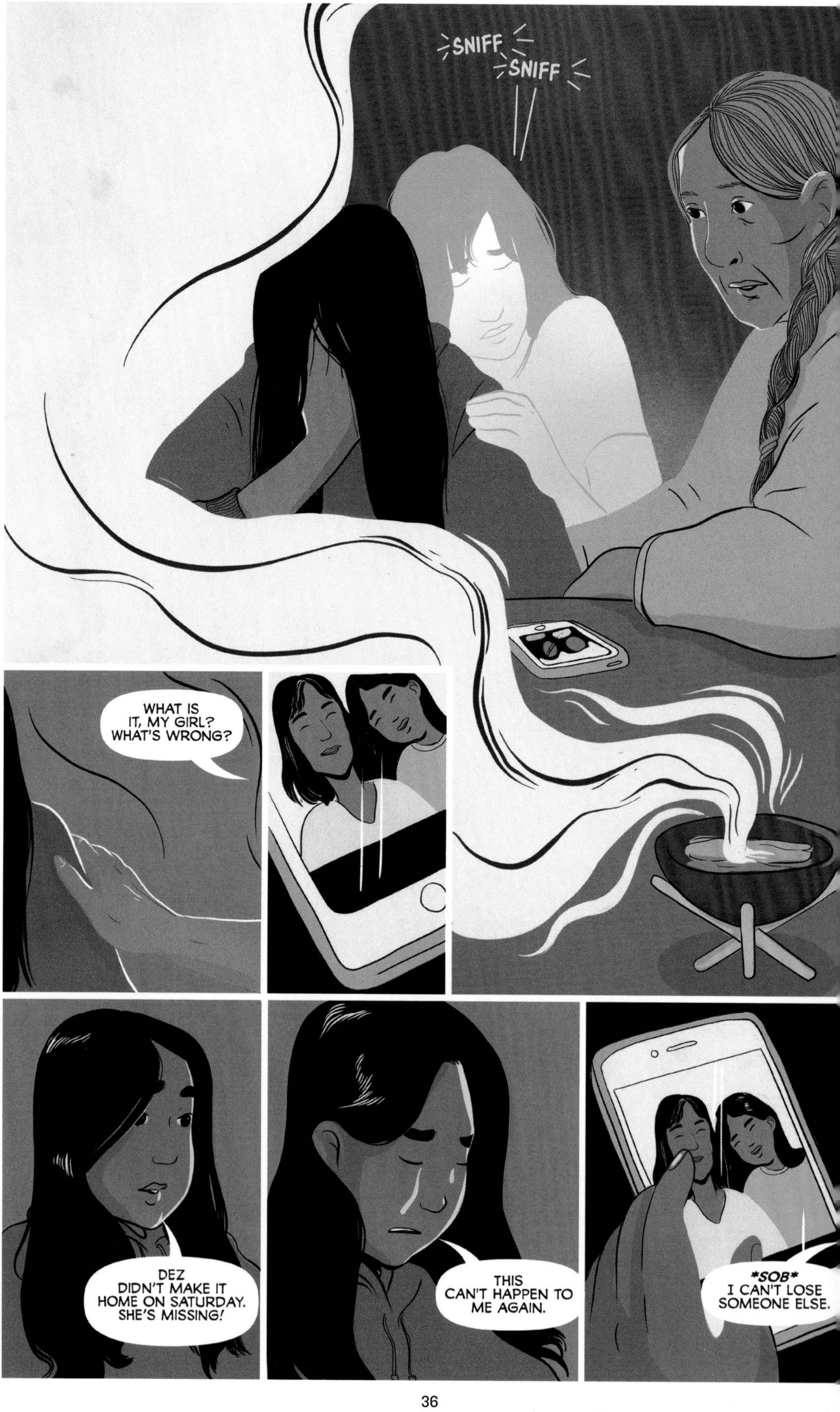
SNIFF
SNIFF
WHAT IS IT, MY GIRL? WHAT'S WRONG?
DEZ DIDN'T MAKE IT HOME ON SATURDAY. SHE'S MISSING!
THIS CAN'T HAPPEN TO ME AGAIN.
SOB I CAN'T LOSE SOMEONE ELSE.

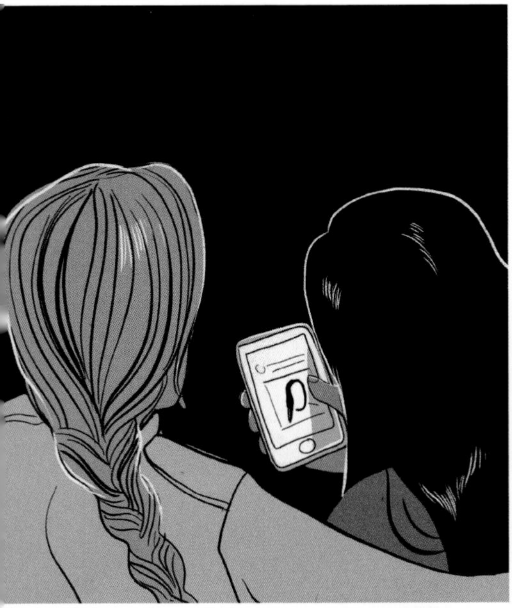

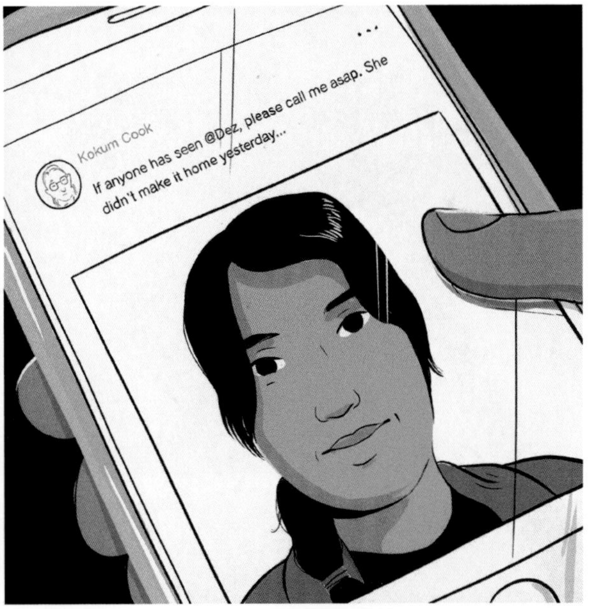
Kokum Cook
If anyone has seen @Dez, please call me asap. She didn't make it home yesterday...

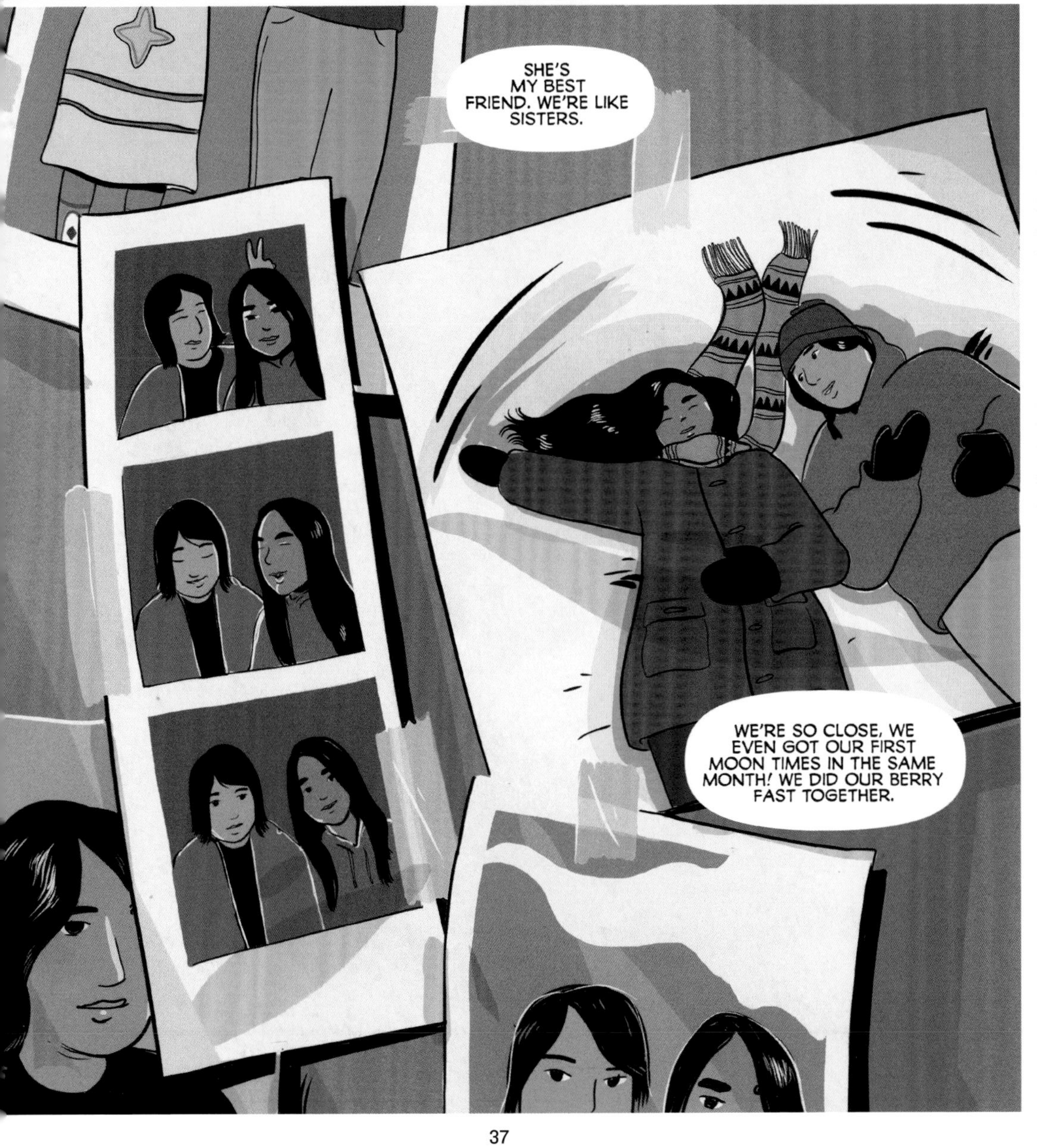
SHE'S MY BEST FRIEND. WE'RE LIKE SISTERS.
WE'RE SO CLOSE, WE EVEN GOT OUR FIRST MOON TIMES IN THE SAME MONTH! WE DID OUR BERRY FAST TOGETHER.

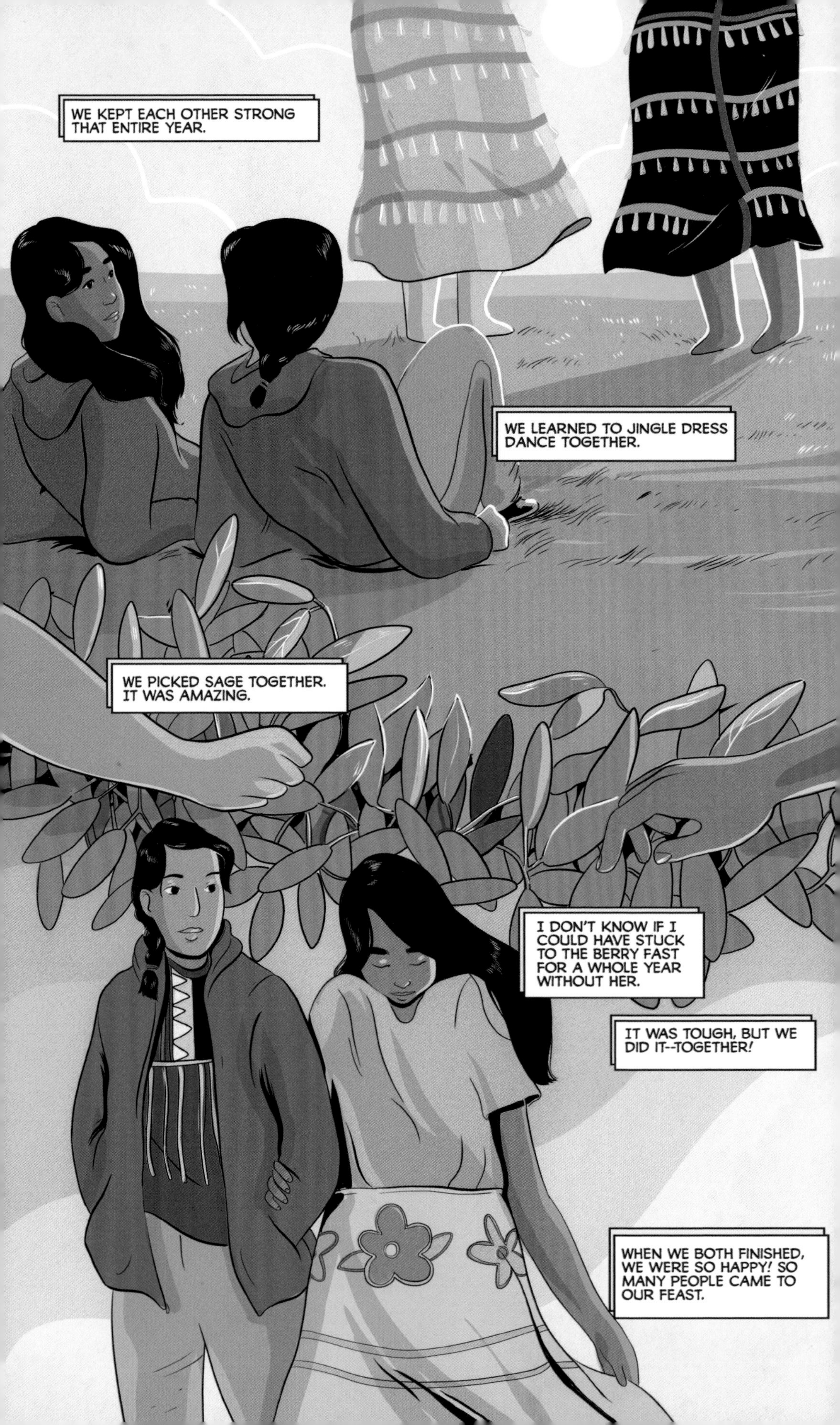
WE KEPT EACH OTHER STRONG THAT ENTIRE YEAR.
WE LEARNED TO JINGLE DRESS DANCE TOGETHER.
WE PICKED SAGE TOGETHER. IT WAS AMAZING.
I DON'T KNOW IF I COULD HAVE STUCK TO THE BERRY FAST FOR A WHOLE YEAR WITHOUT HER.
IT WAS TOUGH, BUT WE DID IT--TOGETHER!
WHEN WE BOTH FINISHED, WE WERE SO HAPPY! SO MANY PEOPLE CAME TO OUR FEAST.

WHEN IT WAS TIME TO BREAK OUR FAST, HER KOKUM GAVE US OUR FIRST BITE OF BERRIES.

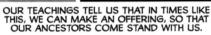

MY MOM WAS STILL WITH US THEN...

OH, MY GIRL, EVERYONE WAS AND STILL IS SO PROUD OF YOU GIRLS!

COMPLETING YOUR BERRY FAST IS A GREAT ACCOMPLISHMENT.

BEING CELEBRATED AS A VALUED PART OF OUR CIRCLE IS AN EXPERIENCE THAT YOU CAN ALWAYS LEAN ON.

I KNOW YOU'RE SCARED RIGHT NOW.

OUR TEACHINGS TELL US THAT IN TIMES LIKE THIS, WE CAN MAKE AN OFFERING, SO THAT OUR ANCESTORS COME STAND WITH US.

DO YOU WANT TO DO THAT?

=SNIFF=

YA, OKAY.

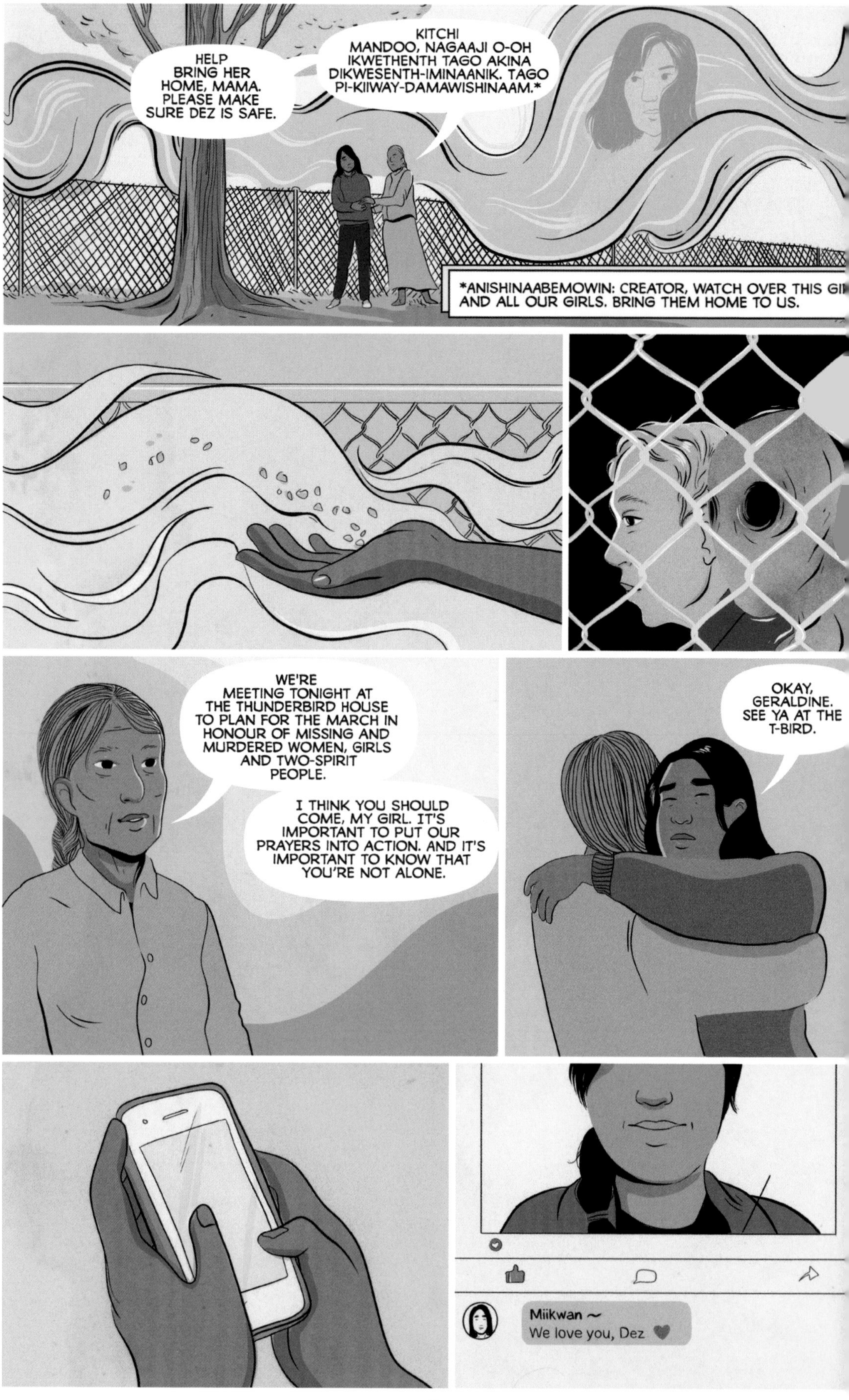
HELP BRING HER HOME, MAMA. PLEASE MAKE SURE DEZ IS SAFE.
KITCHI MANDOO, NAGAAJI O-OH IKWETHENTH TAGO AKINA DIKWESENTH-IMINAANIK. TAGO PI-KIIWAY-DAMAWISHINAAM.*
*ANISHINAABEMOWIN: CREATOR, WATCH OVER THIS GI
AND ALL OUR GIRLS. BRING THEM HOME TO US.
WE'RE MEETING TONIGHT AT THE THUNDERBIRD HOUSE TO PLAN FOR THE MARCH IN HONOUR OF MISSING AND MURDERED WOMEN, GIRLS AND TWO-SPIRIT PEOPLE.
I THINK YOU SHOULD COME, MY GIRL. IT'S IMPORTANT TO PUT OUR PRAYERS INTO ACTION. AND IT'S IMPORTANT TO KNOW THAT YOU'RE NOT ALONE.
OKAY, GERALDINE. SEE YA AT THE T-BIRD.
Miikwan ~
We love you, Dez

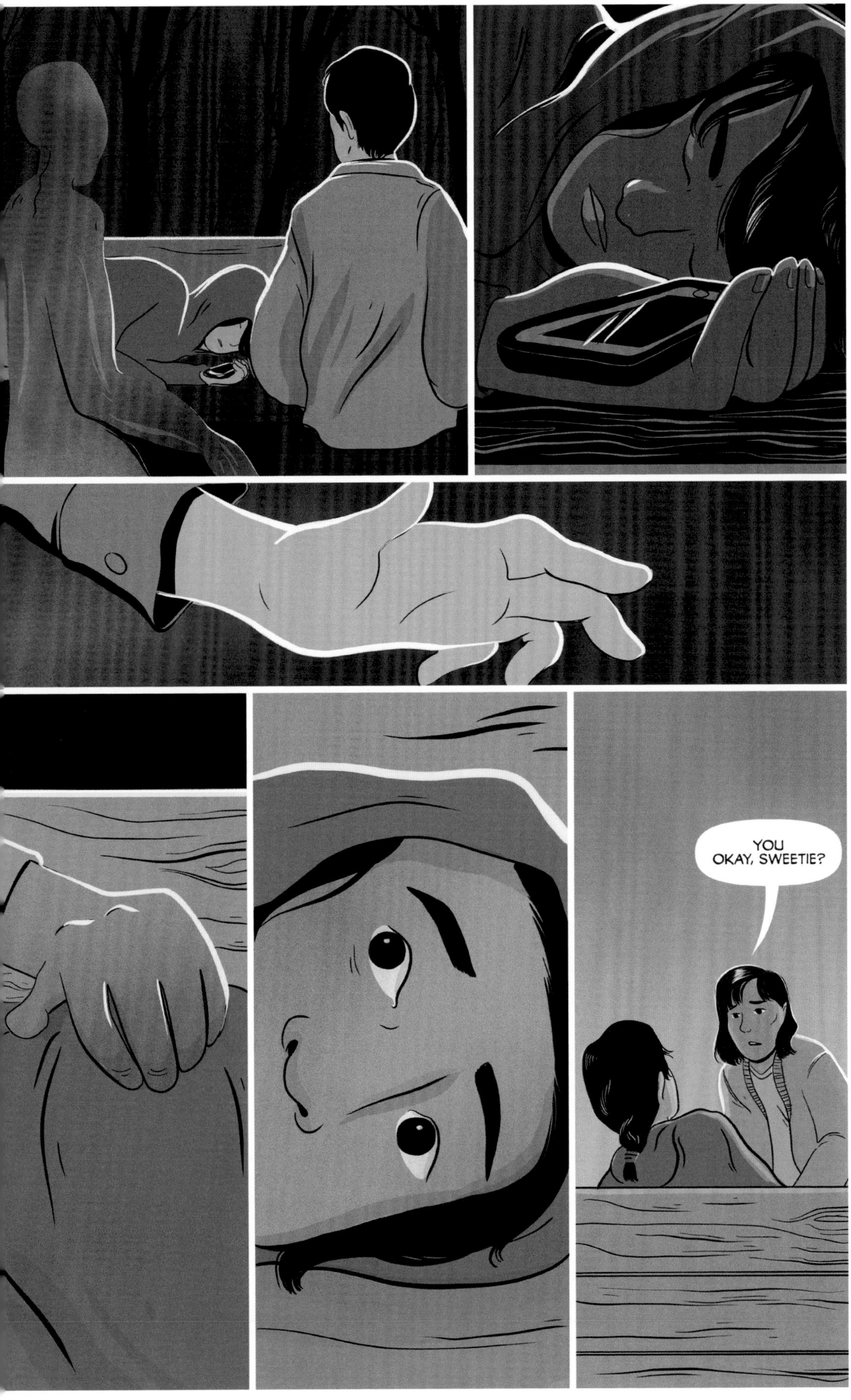
YOU OKAY, SWEETIE?

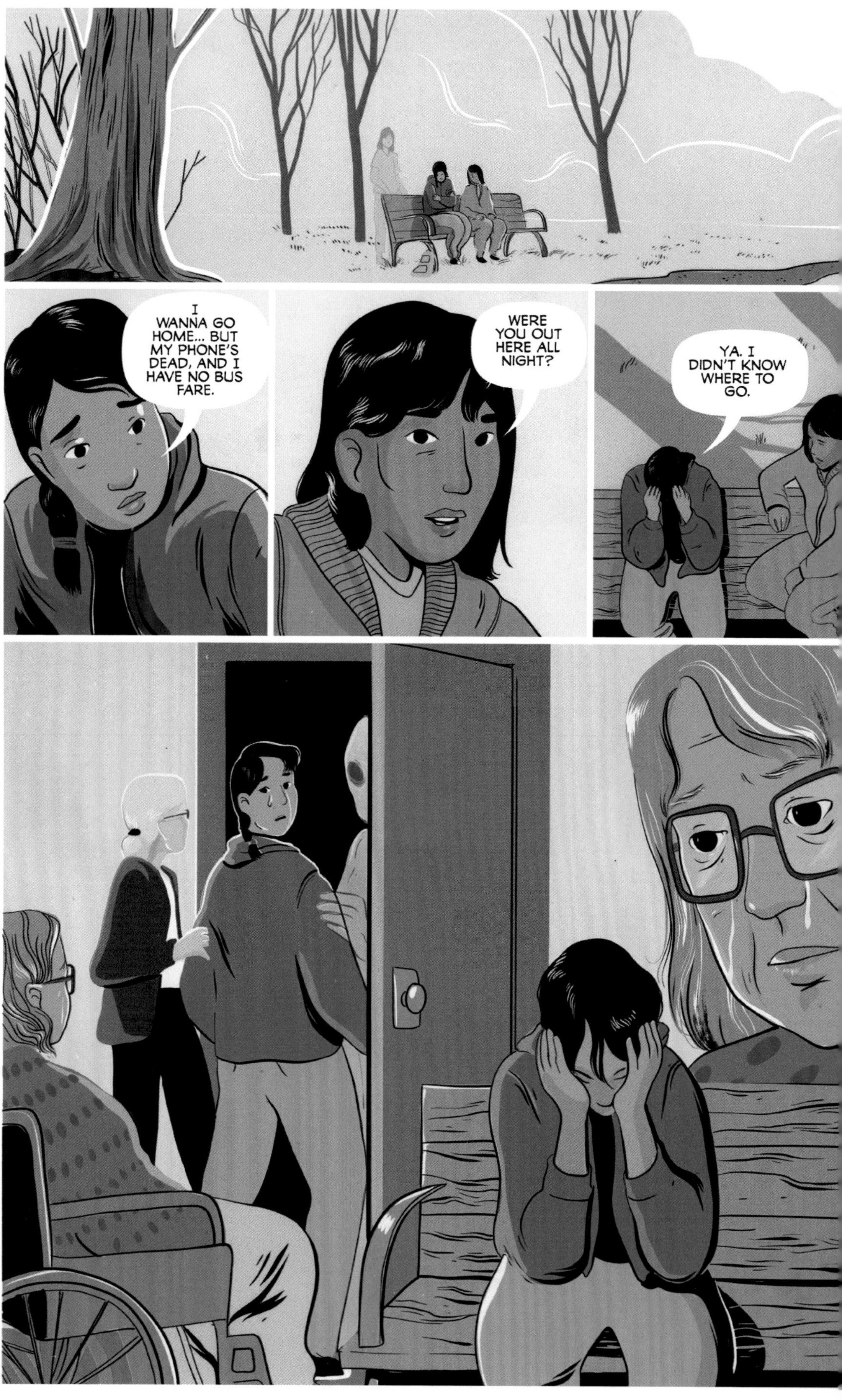
I WANNA GO HOME... BUT MY PHONE'S DEAD, AND I HAVE NO BUS FARE.
WERE YOU OUT HERE ALL NIGHT?
YA. I DIDN'T KNOW WHERE TO GO.

YOU GOTTA BE CAREFUL OUT HERE. IT CAN GET PRETTY ROUGH IN THE CITY.

I KNOW SOMEWHERE YOU CAN USE THE PHONE AND MAYBE GET SOME BUS TICKETS.

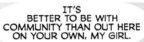

I DON'T WANT TO GO ANYWHERE MY SOCIAL WORKER WILL FIND ME. SHE'S TRYING TO TAKE ME AWAY FROM MY KOKUM.

IT'S NOT LIKE THAT THERE. IT'S COMMUNITY ORGANIZATION RUN BY OUR PEOPLE. THEY CAN HELP OU HOME TO YOUR KOKUM. YOU AN EVEN HAVE A GOOD SMUDGE. AN WALK WITH YOU IF YOU WANT.

I DON'T KNOW--

IT'S BETTER TO BE WITH COMMUNITY THAN OUT HERE ON YOUR OWN, MY GIRL.

MY KOKUM ALWAYS USED TO SAY KAKIYAW NIWAHKOMAKANAK--WE ARE ALL RELATED. SOMETIMES, WE NEED TO LEAN ON ONE ANOTHER FOR SUPPORT. IT'S OKAY TO NEED ONE ANOTHER.

IF THEY CAN HELP ME GET HOME TO MY KOKUM, I'LL CHECK IT OUT.

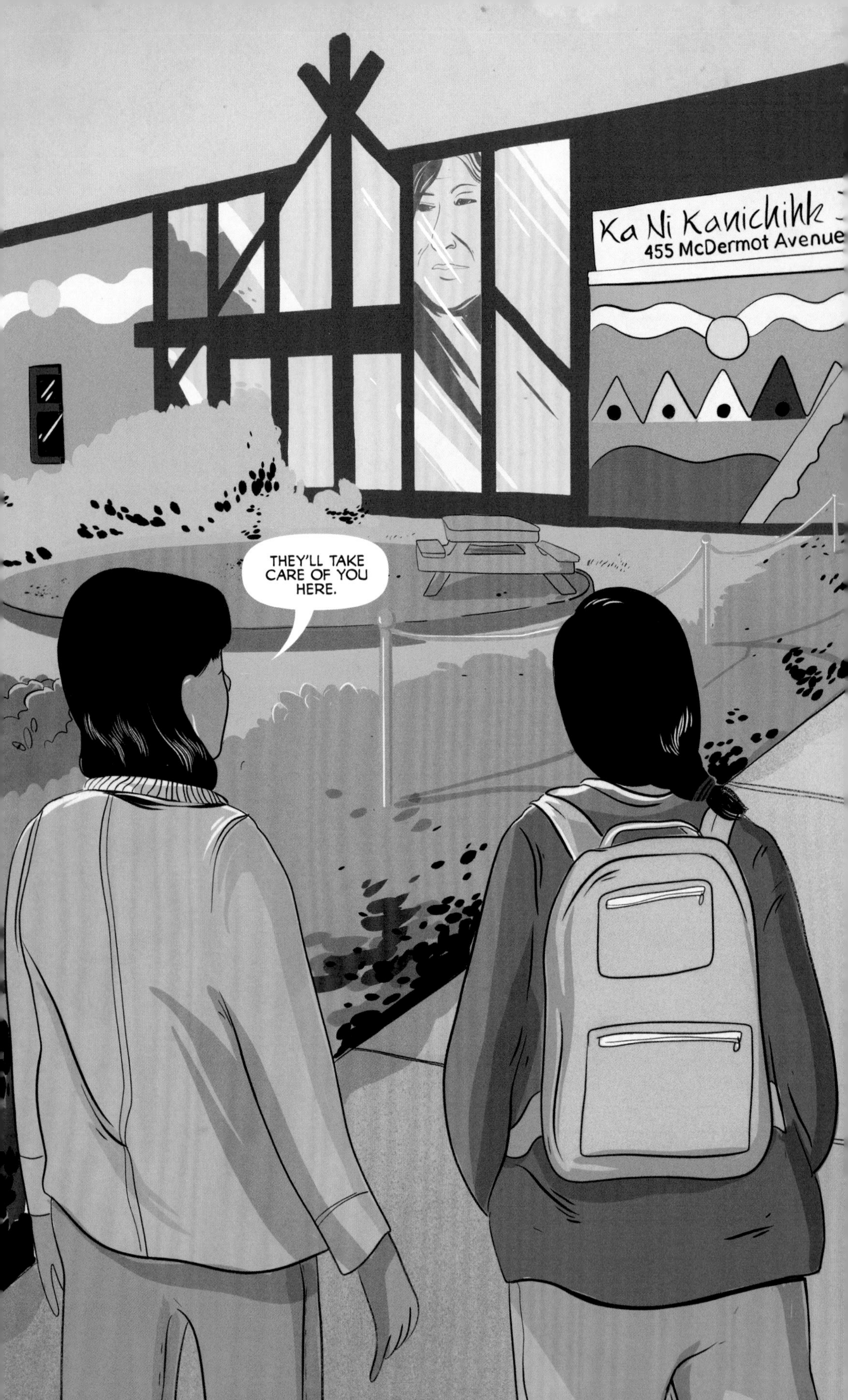
Ka Ni Kanichihk
455 McDermot Avenue
THEY'LL TAKE CARE OF YOU HERE.

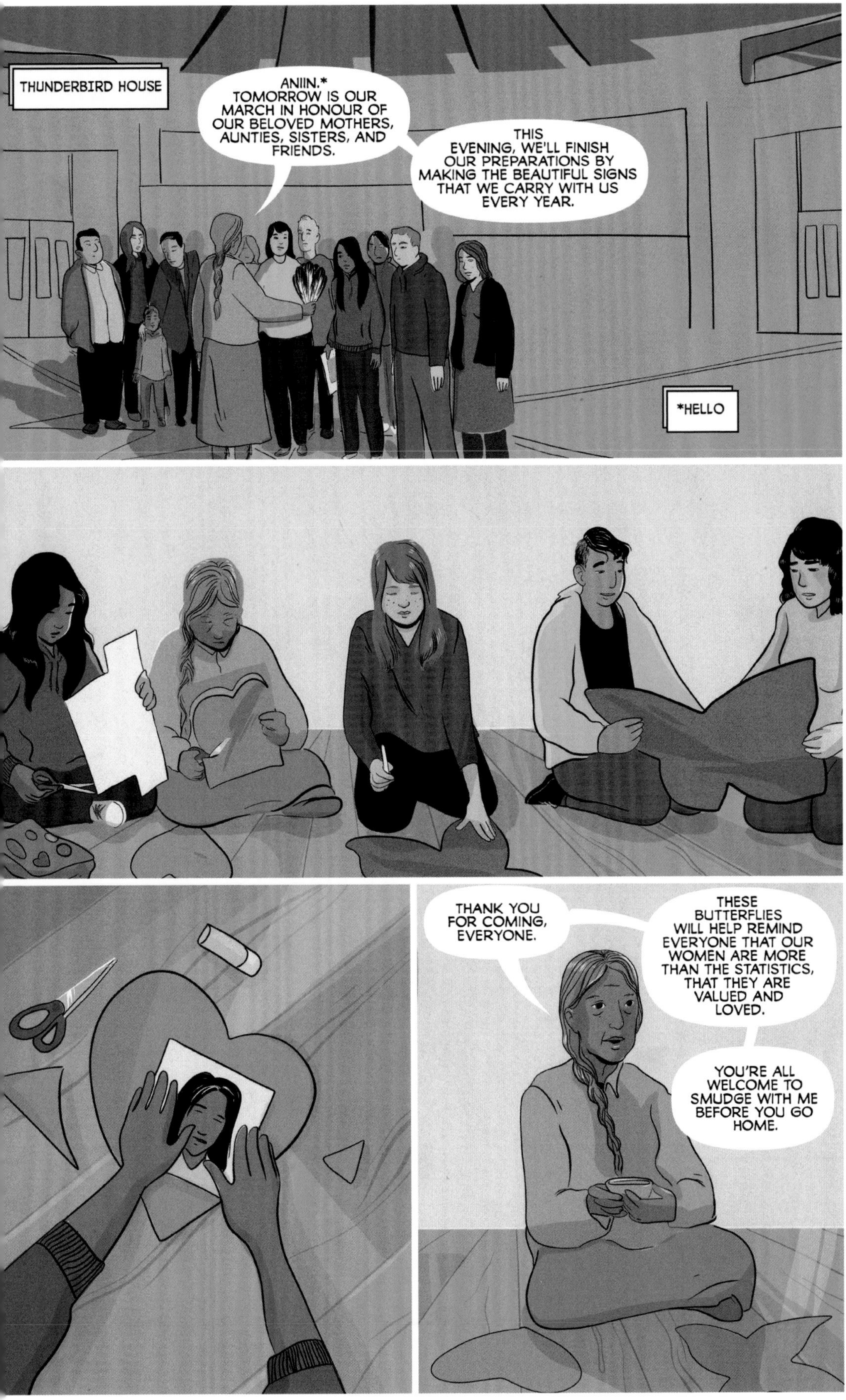
THUNDERBIRD HOUSE
ANIIN.* TOMORROW IS OUR MARCH IN HONOUR OF OUR BELOVED MOTHERS, AUNTIES, SISTERS, AND FRIENDS.
THIS EVENING, WE'LL FINISH OUR PREPARATIONS BY MAKING THE BEAUTIFUL SIGNS THAT WE CARRY WITH US EVERY YEAR.
*HELLO
THANK YOU FOR COMING, EVERYONE.
THESE BUTTERFLIES WILL HELP REMIND EVERYONE THAT OUR WOMEN ARE MORE THAN THE STATISTICS, THAT THEY ARE VALUED AND LOVED.
YOU'RE ALL WELCOME TO SMUDGE WITH ME BEFORE YOU GO HOME.

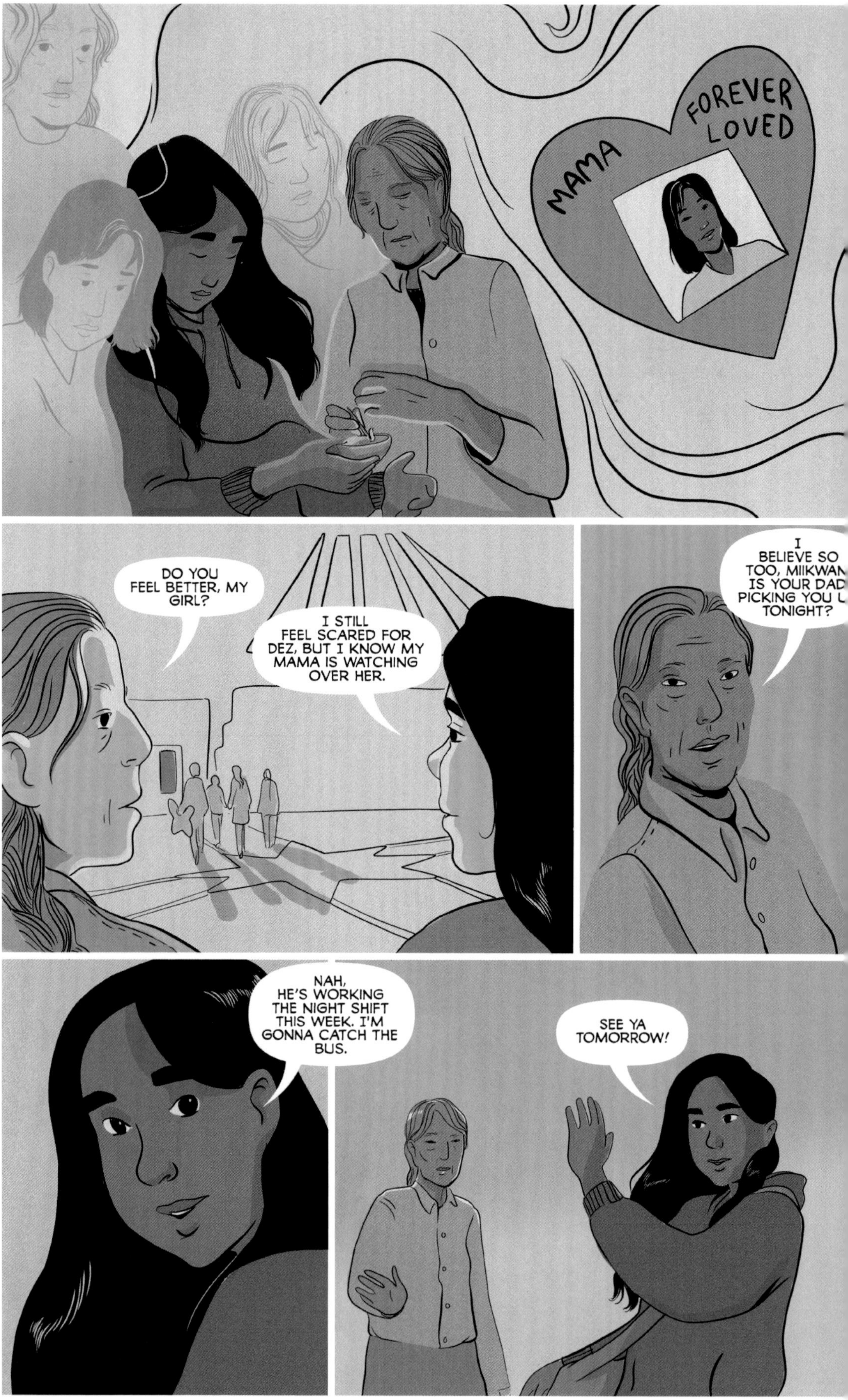
FOREVER LOVED
MAMA
DO YOU FEEL BETTER, MY GIRL?
I STILL FEEL SCARED FOR DEZ, BUT I KNOW MY MAMA IS WATCHING OVER HER.
I BELIEVE SO TOO, MIIKWAN IS YOUR DAD PICKING YOU TONIGHT?
NAH, HE'S WORKING THE NIGHT SHIFT THIS WEEK. I'M GONNA CATCH THE BUS.
SEE YA TOMORROW!

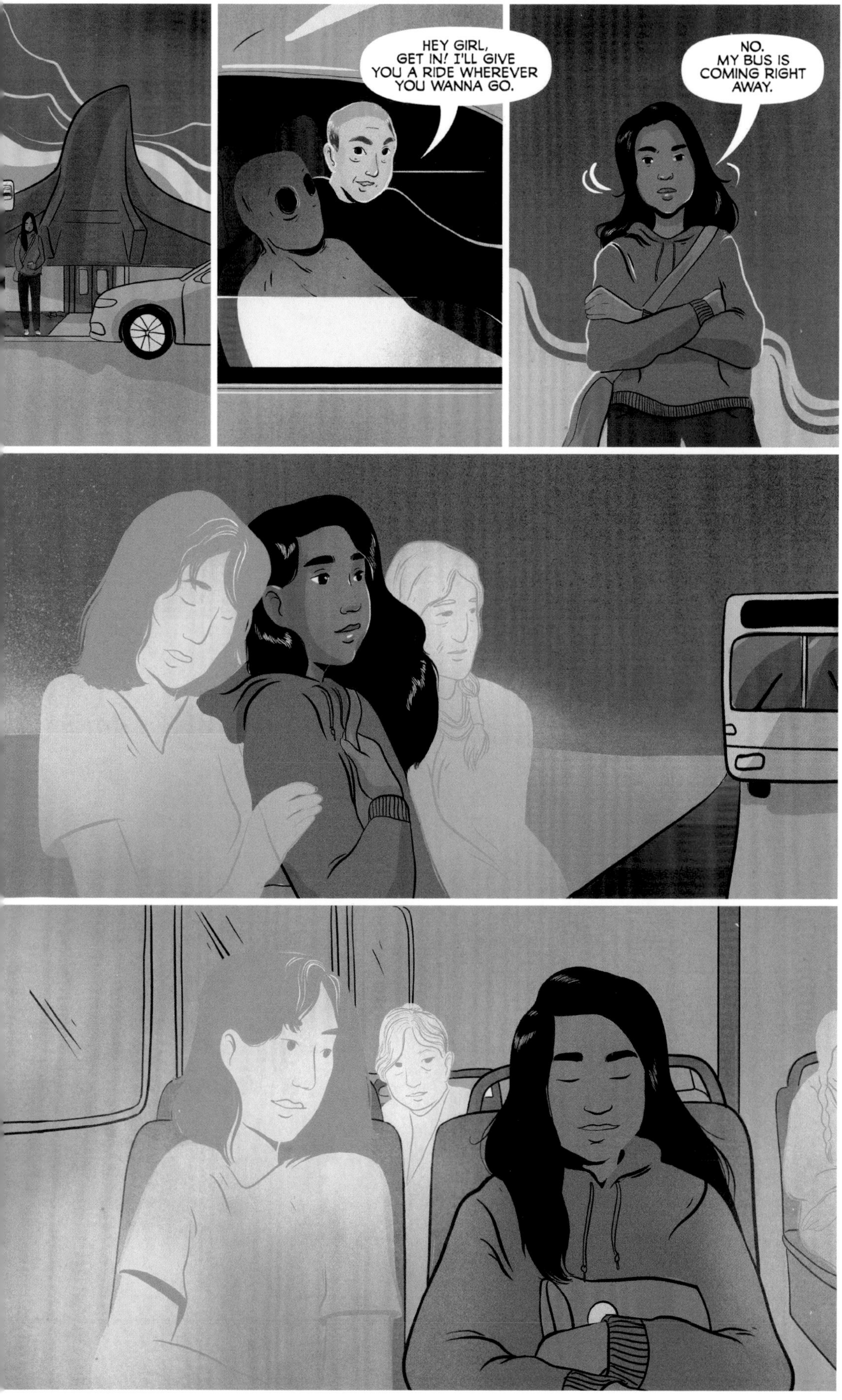
HEY GIRL, GET IN! I'LL GIVE YOU A RIDE WHEREVER YOU WANNA GO.
NO. MY BUS IS COMING RIGHT AWAY.

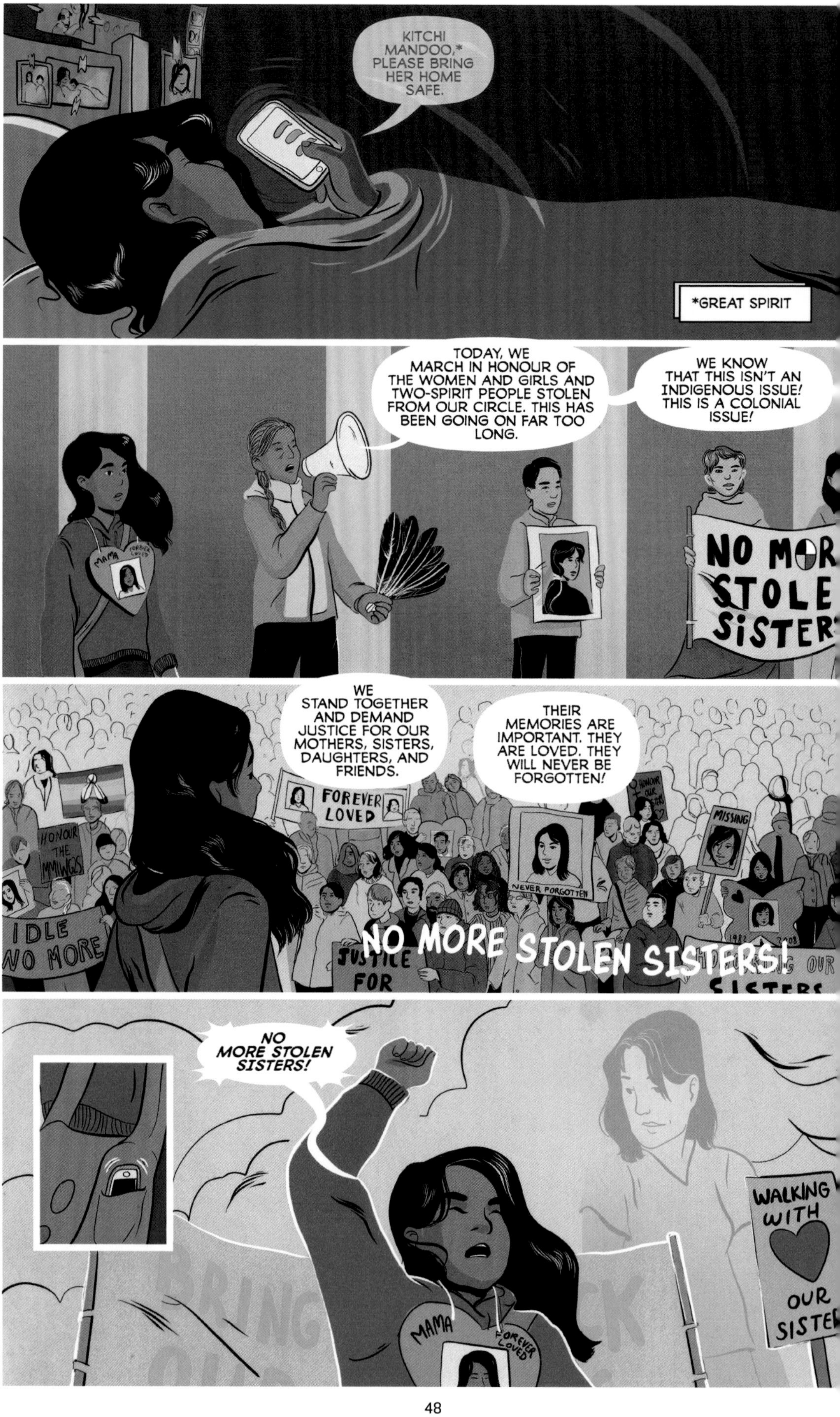
KITCHI MANDOO,* PLEASE BRING HER HOME SAFE.
*GREAT SPIRIT
TODAY, WE MARCH IN HONOUR OF THE WOMEN AND GIRLS AND TWO-SPIRIT PEOPLE STOLEN FROM OUR CIRCLE. THIS HAS BEEN GOING ON FAR TOO LONG.
WE KNOW THAT THIS ISN'T AN INDIGENOUS ISSUE! THIS IS A COLONIAL ISSUE!
MAMA
FOREVER LOVED
NO MORE STOLEN SISTERS
WE STAND TOGETHER AND DEMAND JUSTICE FOR OUR MOTHERS, SISTERS, DAUGHTERS, AND FRIENDS.
THEIR MEMORIES ARE IMPORTANT. THEY ARE LOVED. THEY WILL NEVER BE FORGOTTEN!
FOREVER LOVED
HONOUR THE MMIWG2S
IDLE NO MORE
NEVER FORGOTTEN
MISSING
HONOUR OUR SISTERS
JUSTICE FOR
NO MORE STOLEN SISTERS!
NO MORE STOLEN SISTERS!
WALKING WITH OUR SISTER
MAMA
FOREVER LOVED

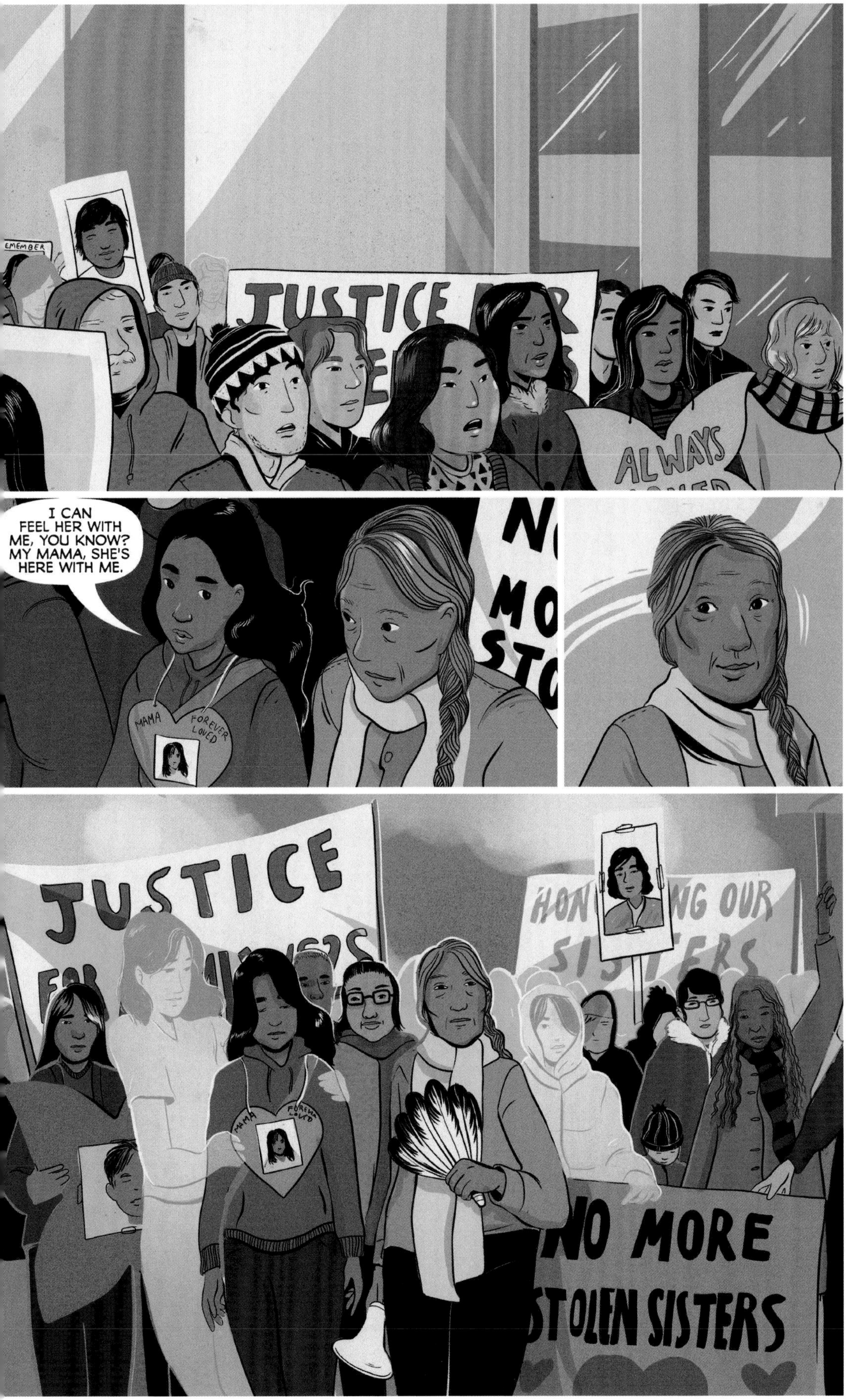
JUSTICE
ALWAYS
I CAN FEEL HER WITH ME, YOU KNOW? MY MAMA, SHE'S HERE WITH ME.
MAMA
FOREVER LOVED
JUSTICE
NO MORE

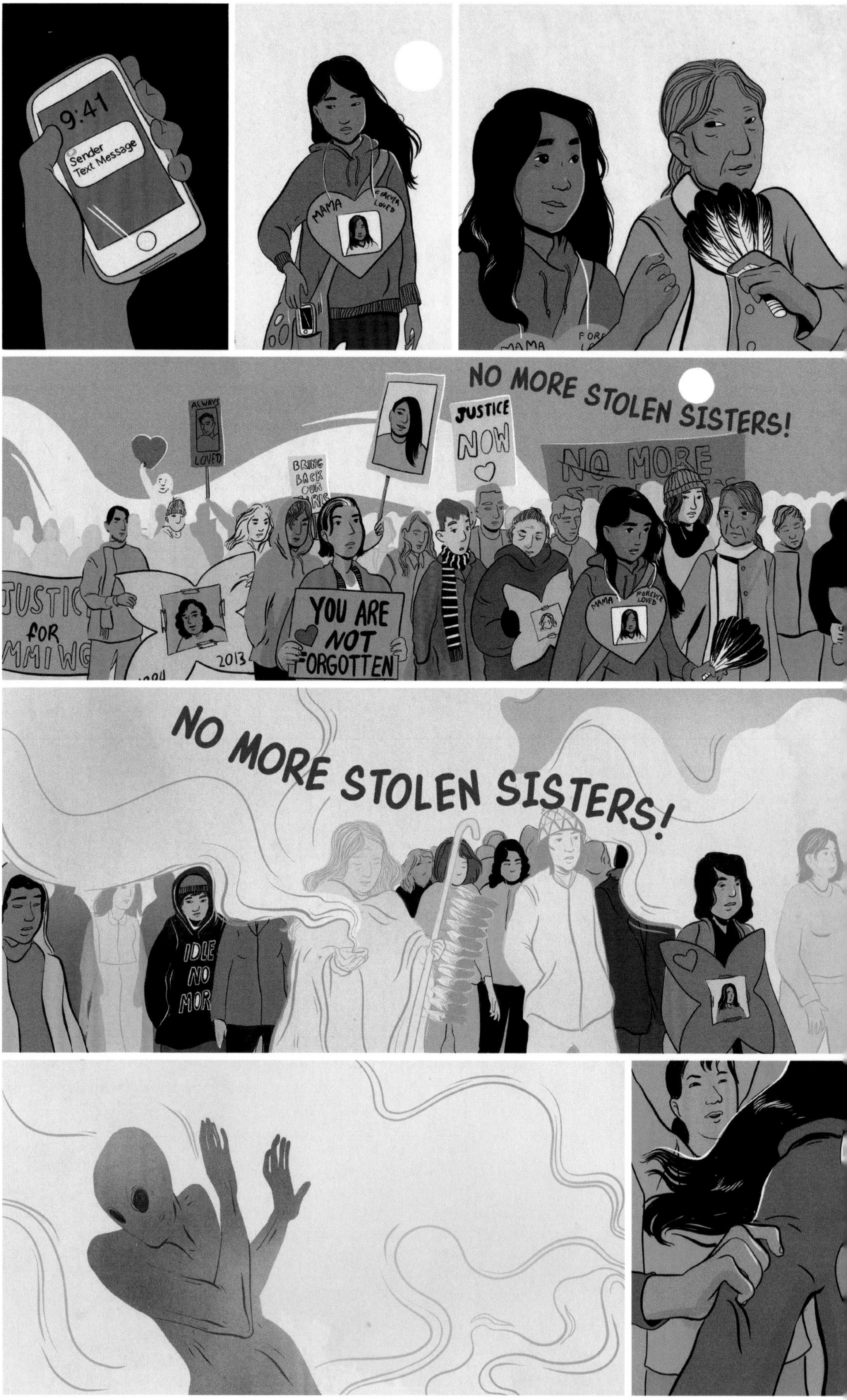
9:41
Sender
Text Message
MAMA
FOREVER LOVED
NO MORE STOLEN SISTERS!
ALWAYS
LOVED
BRING BACK OUR
JUSTICE NOW
NO MORE
JUSTICE FOR MMIWG
2013
YOU ARE NOT FORGOTTEN
MAMA
FOREVER LOVED
NO MORE STOLEN SISTERS!

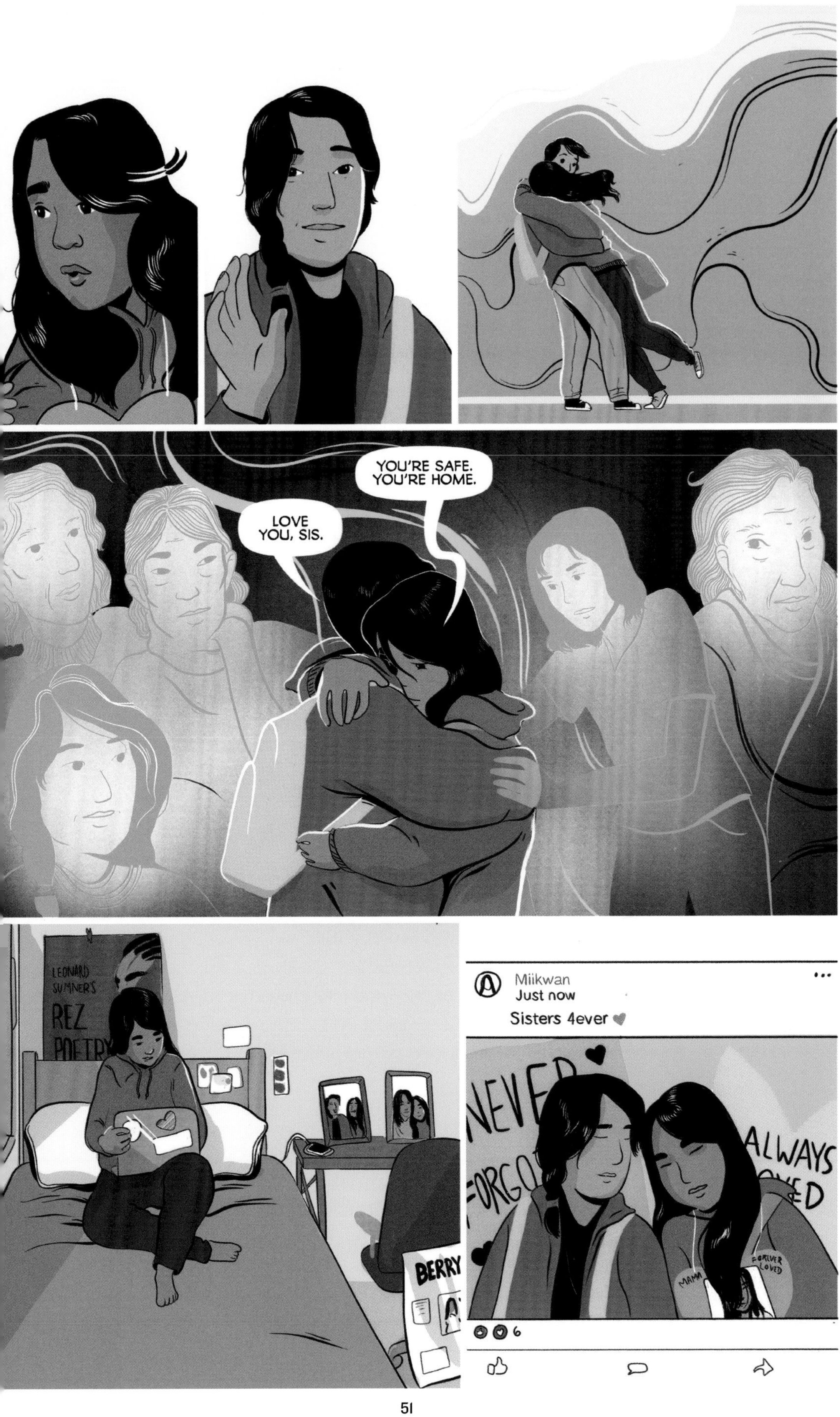
LOVE YOU, SIS.
YOU'RE SAFE. YOU'RE HOME.
LEONARD SUMNER'S
REZ
Miikwan
Just now
Sisters 4ever
MAMA
FOREVER LOVED
6

Murdered and Missing Indigenous Women, Girls, and Two-Spirit People

By Tasha Spillett

As a direct consequence of colonialism, settler capitalism, racism, misogyny, and other forms of oppression, Indigenous women, girls, and two-spirit people are among the most marginalized populations in Canada and globally. We face a greater risk of experiencing racialized and gender-based violence, being murdered, or going missing.

As a part of our refusal of victimhood and in the spirit of resistance, Indigenous women and two-spirit people lead movements against the violence that puts our lives at risk while also healing our communities from the losses we've experienced.

Indigenous women and two-spirit people affirm that our lives are valuable and that we have the right to live on our homelands with respect and dignity, free from violence.

Statistics About MMIWG2S

Indigenous women are five times more likely to be murdered than non-Indigenous women.[1] However, Statistics Canada and several major police forces do not track missing Indigenous women;[2] therefore the following disturbing statistics can only be considered estimates lower than the actual numbers.

According to the Native Women's Association of Canada (NWAC):[3]

- Based on 582 cases of missing and murdered Indigenous women, just over half of the cases (55%) involve women and girls under the age of 31, with 17% of women and girls 18 years of age or younger.
- Nearly half the murder cases in NWAC's database remain unsolved.
- Indigenous women are almost three times more likely to be killed by a stranger than non-Indigenous women.

Of the murder cases in NWAC's database where someone has been charged:

- 16.5% of offenders are strangers with no prior connection to the woman or girl (in contrast, Statistics Canada reports that, between 1997 and 2004, only 6% of murdered non-Indigenous women were killed by strangers);
- 17% of offenders are acquaintances of the woman or girl (a friend, neighbour or someone else known to her); and
- 23% of offenders are a current or former partner of the woman or girl.

According to a 2015 report from the RCMP:[4]

- 10% of women in Canada missing for at least 30 days are Indigenous women.

1 David, Jean-Denis. "Homicide in Canada, 2016." Statistics Canada (website), accessed October 24, 2018, https://www150.statcan.gc.ca/n1/pub/85-002-x/2017001/article/54879-eng.htm

2 Margo McDiarmid, "Still no way to tell how many Indigenous women and girls go missing in Canada each year," CBC (website), CBC News, December 20, 2017, https://www.cbc.ca/news/politics/indigenous-missing-women-police-data-1.4449073.

3 "Fact Sheet: Missing and Murdered Aboriginal Women and Girls," Native Women's Association of Canada (website), Native Women's Association of Canada, accessed October 23, 2018, https://www.nwac.ca/wp-content/uploads/2015/05/Fact_Sheet_Missing_and_Murdered_Aboriginal_Women_and_Girls.pdf.

4 "Missing and Murdered Indigenous Women and Girls," Department of Justice (website), Department of Justice, accessed October 23, 2018, http://justice.gc.ca/eng/rp-pr/jr/jf-pf/2017/july04.html.

- Of these, nearly two-thirds were identified as missing due to "unknown" circumstances, or foul play was suspected.

- Between 1980 and 2014, there were 6,849 police-reported female homicide cases in Canada. 16% of the victims were Indigenous women.

- Since 1991, the number of murdered non-Indigenous women has declined. In contrast, the number of murdered Indigenous women has remained relatively stable, thus accounting for an increasing proportion of Indigenous female homicide victims.

More About MMIWG2S

Altamirano-Jiménez, Isabel. "Indigenous women, nationalism and feminism." *States of Race: Critical Race Feminism for the 21st Century*, edited by S. Razak, M. Smith and S. Thobani, 111-126. Toronto: Between the Lines, 2010.

Beads, Tina and Rauna Kuokkanen. "An Aboriginal Feminist on Violence against Women." *Making Space for Indigenous Feminism*, edited by Joyce Green, 221-232. Winnipeg: Fernwood Publishing, 2007.

Bourassa, Carrie, Kim McKay-McNabb, and Mary Hampton. (2004). "Racism, Sexism and Colonialism: The Impact on the Health of Aboriginal Women in Canada." *Canadian Woman Studies*, 24, no. 1 (2005), 23-29.

Brant, Jennifer and Dawn Memee Lavall-Harvard, *Forever Loved: Exposing the Hidden Crisis of Missing and Murdered Indigenous Women and Girls in Canada*. Bradford, ON: Demeter Press, 2016.

Kuokkanen, Rauna. "Confronting violence: Indigenous women, Self-determination and International Human Rights." *Indivisible: Indigenous Human Rights*, edited by Joyce Green, 126-143. Winnipeg: Fernwood Press, 2014.

Palmater, Pam. "The Law's Role in Canada's Disgrace: Murdered & Missing Indigenous Women & Girls" EquitableEducation. Retrieved October 23, 2018: https://www.youtube.com/watch?v=6g665LSQpX0.

"Stolen Sisters: A Human Rights Response to Discrimination and Violence against Indigenous Women in Canada," Amnesty International (website), Amnesty International, accessed October 23, 2018, https://www.amnesty.ca/sites/amnesty/files/amr200032004enstolensisters.pdf.

Tuck, Eve and K. Wayne Yang (2012). "Decolonization is not a metaphor." *Decolonization: Indigeneity, Education & Society*, 1 no. 1 (2012), 1-40.

"Violence Against Indigenous Women and Girls in Canada: A Summary of Amnesty International's Concerns and Call to Action," Amnesty International (website), Amnesty International, last modified February 7, 2014, https://www.amnesty.ca/sites/amnesty/files/iwfa_submission_amnesty_international_february_2014_-_final.pdf.

Walker, Connie, "Who Killed Alberta Williams," CBC Radio (website), CBC Radio, February 24, 2015, https://www.cbc.ca/news/politics/indigenous-missing-women-police-data-1.4449073.

Further Reading

Adams, K.C. *Perception Photo Series*. Winnipeg, MB: HighWater Press, 2019.

Clements, Marie. *The Edward Curtis Project: A Modern Picture Story*. Vancouver, BC: Talonbooks, 2010.

Dimaline, Cherie. *The Marrow Thieves*. Toronto, ON: Dancing Cat Books, 2017.

Dumont, Marilyn. *A Really Good Brown Girl*. London, ON: Brick Books, 2015.

Justice, Daniel Heath. *The Way of Thorn & Thunder, Vol. 1-3*. Neyaashiinigmiing, ON: Kegedonce Press, 2016.

Mosionier, Beatrice. *In Search of April Raintree*. Winnipeg, MB: Portage & Main Press, 2008.

Robertson, David A. *Betty: The Helen Betty Osborne Story*. Winnipeg, MB: HighWater Press, 2016.

Robertson, David A. *Will I See?* Winnipeg, MB: HighWater Press, 2017.

Storm, Jennifer. *Deadly Loyalties*. Penticton, BC: Theytus Books, 2007.

Taylor, Drew Hayden. *The Night Wanderer: A Graphic Novel*. Toronto, ON: Annick Press, 2013.

Vermette, Katherena. *A Girl Called Echo, Vol. 1-4*. Winnipeg, MB: HighWater Press, 2017-2020.